JUST HIS IMAGINATION...

The heated water rinsed his hair and ran down his slippery skin. The pain in his head actually seemed to wash away with the soap. He twisted off the water. Quiet. Dripping, he opened the shower curtain, stepped out onto the fringed bathmat and pulled the curtain closed again.

The air in the bathroom had turned to a regular murky-white London fog from the shower steam. Gabe began to dry himself with a big orange towel. He worked the towel through his wet hair, across his neck and chest, and then down to his...

The two fists exploded through the shower curtain on either side of Gabe. For a slice of a second Gabe saw green then blackness as the hands clamped onto his face from behind, like two huge spiders. Gabe clawed at the white air as he was jerked off his feet...

LEE J. HINDLE
DRAGON FALL

AN AVON FLARE BOOK

DRAGON FALL is an original publication of Avon
Books. This work has never before appeared in book
form. This work is a novel. Any similarity to actual per-
sons or events is purely coincidental.

AVON BOOKS
A division of
The Hearst Corporation
1790 Broadway
New York, New York 10019

First Flare Printing, November, 1984

FLARE TRADEMARK REG. U.S. PAT. OFF. AND IN
OTHER COUNTRIES, MARCA REGISTRADA,
HECHO EN U.S.A.

Printed in the U.S.A.

WFH 10 9 8 7 6 5 4 3 2 1

For Marie Marguerite Adelaide Elaine
"Are you finished that thing, yet?" Hindle:
My mom. She kept me going.

Life does not consist mainly —or even largely—of facts and happenings. It consists mainly of the storm of thoughts that is forever blowing through one's head.

—Mark Twain

DRAGONFALL

One

Silence.

Cool and crystalline.

Gabriel Holden, five going on six, was lost in sleep. He lay on his side, curled up tight under his massive bedcovers. His small form rose and fell with his breathing.

A noise. Tapping in the darkness.

Gabe didn't hear.

It got louder.

Gabe opened an eye halfway.

It stopped.

Gabe closed his eye.

It started again.

Gabe opened his eye again.

It stopped again.

The little boy rolled over and faced the wall, his back to the room.

Silence.

Then, ever so slowly, a low liquid growling rose from out of the silence, from out of the night, from out of his closet.

He rolled back around, eyes wide, to face the closed doors of his closet, his lips pursed and quivering.

Then, to add to his terror, the folding doors opened a crack. He stared as a pearly knife poked through the opening. Then another one appeared alongside it. And another one.

Gabe's eyes ballooned as he realized they weren't knives at all. They were fingernails.

He didn't need to see any more. The boy was up, out and down the dingy mile-long hallway as fast as his little pumping legs would go. He made first-time contact with the knob of his parents' closed bedroom door and spilled in. He jumped blindly onto the bed and gained sanctuary between Mommy and Daddy.

"Whut—"

"Who—"

"Gabriel?"

"It's Gabriel."

The table lamp on Mommy's side clicked on. Gabe was underneath the covers up to his eyeballs.

"There's s-ss-something in my . . . closet . . . a m-monster . . . or ah-I-I dunno . . . it was something, I saw it!"

He started to cry, warm tears bubbling over. Mommy hugged him to her.

"Bad dream, Gabe, only a bad dream. That's all it was," she soothed.

"Nuh-no-no, Mommy. I was awake, wide awake. I was!"

Daddy stood up with a grunt and came around the bed.

"C'mon, Gabe. Lessgo," he said.

"No, Daddy! It—it's . . . in there! It growled at me an'—"

"Nothing growled at you, Gabe. It's all up there," Daddy said, tapping Gabe's temple. "Now, c'mon, I'll show you."

"Gabe can stay here," Mommy said, powder-

12

soft. "He's not going to get any sleep tonight now that he—"

"Nobody's going to get any sleep at all if we don't stop this stupid thing right now. Lessgo, buster."

Daddy scooped Gabe upside down in his left arm.

"No, Daddy! Don't! I don't wanna go back! It's there! It's really there an'—Mommeeeeeeee!"

Mommy started to get up.

"No, Marie, just stay. I'll be done in a minute," Daddy said, and carried the blubbering Gabriel down the dark hallway.

Daddy turned on the big light in Gabe's room and dropped him in front of the closet.

"Something in the closet, right?" Daddy asked wearily.

Gabe quickly backpedaled away from the closet doors, pulling up his drooping pajama bottoms.

"Yeah, it was tapping and . . . and growling . . . in there. I heard it. It started to come out."

"Right," Daddy said in a louder voice. "Let's take a look-see."

"No, no, NO, Daddy! Don't! Don't! DON'T!"

Daddy whipped the doors open. "Voilà!"

Gabe clapped his hands to his face. Nothing happened. He peered through two fingers, looking past Daddy into that vault of infinite darkness. Nothing.

Daddy stood in front of the open closet with his hands on his hips, facing Gabe.

"There, you see, Gabe? Nothing. It was all up in your noggin. All of it. It was your I-M-A-G-I—uh—N-A-T-I-O-N. Your silly imagination. That's all. 'Kay, sport?"

Gabe's small body went to rubber with relief. He forced a tiny pink smile for Daddy.

"Right, now, let's get you back into the sack."

Daddy put his left foot forward as the two huge, gnarled arms coated in a slick black goo shot out and circled around him in a steel hug. Daddy was a blur as he was jerked back into the closet. The metal doors boomed shut after him.

Silence.

Gabe just stood there, hands dangling at his sides. His eyes were glass saucers. He opened his mouth slowly, heavily, and then he screamed. Long and hard.

The scream eased into an intense, even buzzing.

Gabriel Holden, seventeen going on eighteen, jerked awake from the dream and fell out of bed.

K-PHUMP!

"Holy sheep-dip, that was interesting."

York laughed. It was a silent, frozen laugh. That was the only kind he had. He was leaning up against the closed bedroom door, hands behind him. He had on a yellow Coors Beer T-shirt and cutoffs.

Gabe brought his hand down on the buzzing clock radio.

Another nightmare. For the last six weeks it was always the same. It was always his family meeting their ends in some horrible, bizarre manner. In the last couple of weeks the dreams had steadily worsened. Dad was the first, then Mom, then his older sister, Rachel, and his little brother, Tyler. This morning Dad had bought it again. But it was never Gabe. Not yet.

With a flick of his middle finger he switched from ALARM over to RADIO.

"—et the down-to-earth facts you need right now. Shop the way of the future. Call Alpha-Star Computer Info today. That's Alpha-Star-2001. And please, get your own dates."

"Wasn't that a thrill. And a good, good Sunday morn to you too. This is J-KLM, the radio station that's never out of order. And this is Cameron Sly sitting in for Robbie Breeze who, confidentially, *is* out of order. Has been since birth. All right, for those of you who are still into that time thing, it's twenty after nine and I've got three in a row starting off with that foppish quintet from jolly ol' England, Duran Duran."

Gabe lazily pulled himself up onto his bed. He stared down at his bare feet. His illustrated feet, he called them. Because they were. Intricately detailed black felt pen drawings covered his feet, even his soles. Pictures of sunrises, sunsets, space shuttles, samurai, and a voluptuous vampire drooling blood. They started at his little toe and ended just above his ankle. Gabe draws on his feet.

He squinted. The bright morning sun had already begun its hieroglyphics on the walls in his room. He smacked his lips.

"Eeesh, morning breath. The worst."

Sid laughed. It, too, was frozen and silent. The only kind he had. He sat on top of Gabe's desk with his arm on Gabe's little color Sony. He wore a red muscle shirt and plaid shorts.

Gabe's room was in general disarray. Papers, candy wrappers, open magazines, and bits of clothing were assigned to different spots in the room. Dirty glasses and plates were sitting everywhere. It looked like a graveyard where old dishes go to die.

He had fallen asleep with his clothes on again. He had been staying up late a lot lately, working long after midnight in his room. He knew sleeping in his clothes was unhealthy for him in some way—lack of oxygen to the skin or something like that. Flawlessly lip-synching the frenzied lyrics from the radio, he stretched wide and pulled off his white T-shirt. He reached around and scratched his back grizzly-style, his nails raking his spine.

Gabe was a tall boy, and in the past months he had worked up from skinny to slender through custard doughnuts, milkshakes, and off-and-on bouts with his barbells. He also did a lot of ten-speed biking and had earned a light tan from the outdoor effort. Thick black hair, parted at the left and feathered back unevenly, framed his narrow, serious face.

Gabe stepped toward his varnished dresser to get a fresh shirt and felt a definite squish under his right foot. He looked down and discovered he had stepped on a forgotten half of a crunchy pea-nut butter and peach yogurt sandwich. He lifted his sticky foot too quickly and smashed his toes into his desk.

"Ack! Blaspheme. Curse. Swear. Cuss, cuss."

Hubub laughed. Frozen and silent. The only kind he had. He sat on the metal stool at Gabe's drafting table with his elbows propped up behind him. He wore just a crumpled pair of flow-ery Jamaican shorts.

Hubub had come into existence third. He had the bulkiest build of the three, a sumo-wrestler's stature. Sid had been second. His massive arms hung down almost to his knees, giving him an ape-like posture. York held his head high and had more of a defined build than his two companions. He had been the first of the three.

Each stood just over five feet on short, powerful legs. Each possessed enormously muscled arms and a well-developed chest. They had the same stony, brooding expression on their large faces. Their broad, slightly open mouths, filled with rows of jagged triangular teeth, were shaped into what could be described as grimaces of pain.

For what it's worth, they weren't always like that. No, they were very different once.

Made of fiberglass, deep foam, wire mesh, and the finest latex around, they all viewed the world through blood-colored glass eyeballs; all stitched, glued, and joined together with meticulous care by the hands of their originator, their maker, their creator: the young man known as Gabriel Holden. Gabe calls them his "boys."

Bumping York out of the way, Gabe hopped down the hallway to the bathroom. Having washed his limb, he ran the toothbrush over his teeth, grabbed a blue T-shirt with NIGHT OF THE LIVING DEAD across it from his top dresser drawer, picked up his khaki-green jacket, and bounded softly downstairs. He was going to be late for work.

It was Sunday morning and the rest of the Holden family wasn't up yet.

He skidded across the kitchen on the light brown linoleum floor and whipped open the fridge door. He chose a boysenberry yogurt and gulped it down in two swallows. He tossed the empty cup into the garbage pail under the kitchen sink, then spun on his heel and reached into the pantry that was lodged between the refrigerator and the broad kitchen counter. He

17

seized a pack of Mr. Christie's Raspberry-Filled Oatmeal Cookies and made for the front door.

Beneath rumpled blue jeans, muscular legs pumped furiously up and down. Gabe picked up his pace as he pedaled down Landau Street which, along with the sidewalks, parks, and places of business, was empty.

It was Sunday morning and the rest of the city was still asleep.

He was on a ten-speed bicycle, a wine-colored machine that Gabe had bought, like the majority of other young males, with the income earned from a long-forgotten paper route.

At the end of Landau, he turned left and went down Eleventh Avenue, heading for Port Street. He rode in and out of the long, cool shadows the morning sun hadn't yet illumined. Reaching Port, he sailed around a bend and crossed over Irons Bridge. Three and a half blocks up he coasted onto the cracked sidewalk and locked his bicycle to a flaking metal rack in front of the Speller Townhouse Groceteria.

The little silver bell over the door jingled as Gabe quickly stepped into the quiet store. He inhaled the smell of the place. It was a special blend of metal, tile, and dust.

Mr. Joyoki, the boss and owner, stood waiting at the Formica counter between the cash register and the paper-thin boxes of root beer jawbreakers, seven-foot licorice whips, purple piggy chew-bombs, and other assorted pieces of refined sugar. He was a chunky Japanese man bordering on the big fifty and had wispy black hair that he kept greased back from his round, beefy face. He wore thick-rimmed glasses that teetered on the tip of his nose.

Taking off his jacket, Gabe raced up to the counter.

"You're late," Mr. Joyoki said.

"Sorry," Gabe said.

"I had to wait for you."

"Sorry."

"Got a reason?"

"Heavy traffic."

"On a Sunday morning?"

"Pilgrimage to Mecca."

Mr. Joyoki waved a pudgy hand, pushing the comment away, and came around the counter.

"Just don't let it become a habit for you," he said.

"Don't worry 'bout it," Gabe said, going around to the business side of the counter.

"I do. Fill up the pet food shelf and the fridge. It's going to be slow today, so you'll have lots of time. Bye."

"Wait. Mr. Joyoki? By any chance, can I get next Saturday off? My cousin is getting married over in—"

Mr. Joyoki was shaking his head quickly.

"No can do, Gabe. Taking the family on a little holiday next weekend. Missed my chance in the summer. I'm gonna need you all weekend. It'll be just you and Sam. You'll be here, okay?"

"Yeah, fine."

Gabe shrugged. He didn't care. He didn't want to go to the wedding anyway. He didn't get along at all with Richard, the young groom-to-be. Wimpy, crater-faced, sewer-mouthed Richard. Ever since Gabe was old enough to see the obvious in people he had known Mom's nephew to fit that bill to a lecherous T. And now he was

19

getting married. "That poor, poor girl," Gabe had said when he heard the news. "Damnation is putting it mildly."

Mr. Joyoki went to the far end of the counter and hoisted two hefty boxes up into his arms.

"Okay. Angela'll be in at five. Bye," he said, and left by the back door.

Angela'll be in at five, Gabe said to himself. Ah, Angela. A female to be wary of, for sure.

Gabe always tried to think of a word that would properly describe Mr. Joyoki's sixteen-year-old daughter. *Promiscuous, lewd, risqué,* and/or *bike* never seemed to fit. She was just . . . Angela, and she had the undeniable capability to turn a young man's sturdy legs into Aunt Jemima's Waffle Mix.

It was a hair after noon and Gabe was painfully bored. He had counted, filled, arranged, and cleaned everything that didn't move and a couple of things that did. Painfully bored. He didn't even want customers to break up the monotony. He just wanted his beloved shift to be over and done with so that he could get out of there. He had somewhere to go tonight.

He swiveled around on his high padded stool and clicked on the little black radio that Mr. Joyoki kept on the windowsill beside the October issues of *Penthouse, Hustler,* and *Oui.* He turned up the volume. Jackson Browne was running on empty.

Suspended cheek to cheek from the wooden rim at the top of the window were the latest in Halloween goodies. A conglomeration of full-head masks of only the best natural latex rubber. Ranging in price from $4.99 to $129.99, the

miniature gallery included the gothic Werew[...]
of London, a blue-in-the-face Tusken Raider, th[...]
endearing Mutating Face, and finally and ulti-
mately, a mask that actually looked like refrig-
erated puke with nostrils. Good stuff, folks.

Gabe gazed out the store window. A middle-
aged gentleman was walking down the sidewalk across the street. He stepped off the curb
and began to cross over to the store. Gabe
started his game.

"No," Gabe said. "Stop."

The man kept walking.

"No! Stop right there! Don't come any closer!
Not a step, not a . . . No! Stop! Right there!
Don't you dare! Don't you— Stop it! Stop!" Gabe
yelled at the man through the glass window.

The man was almost in front of the store.

"Hey, I mean it! I said stop! Halt! *Basta!*
RIGHT NOW! STOP! PLEASE! THERE'S A
BOMB TIED TO THE DOOR AND IF YOU
OPEN IT— NO! NO!! NOOOOOOO!"

The little silver bell on the door jingled as the
man stepped into the quiet store.

Gabe smiled at him.

"Good afternoon," he said cheerily.

Twenty minutes of two o'clock. Gabe was
hunched on the counter re-re-reading the latest
issue of *Fangoria* when the kid walked in. He
had tangled red hair and wore a baggy white
jacket and violet jeans. He darted a look at Gabe
and disappeared around the bakery shelf at the
rear of the groceteria. Gabe went back to his
magazine, then looked up again to see where
the kid had gotten to. He was coming up the
aisle, heading for Gabe. He quickly scanned the

21

candy counter, picked out a purple piggy chew-bomb, flicked down a quarter, and had started for the door when Gabe got around the counter in front of him. The kid's face came up to Gabe's chest and had "I did it" smeared all over it.

"Y'okay, Scarface, let's have it," Gabe said, holding out his hand.

The kid backed up a step.

"Have what?" the kid asked with a frown.

"The goods, smoothie. C'mon." He pointed to the new bulge in the kid's jacket.

"Don't know what you're talkin' about," the kid said, now annoyed.

"Oh. Ooohh, I'm sorry. Hey, I didn't know. When are you *expecting?*" Gabe asked, patting the bulge. In a burst of movement he stuffed both hands into the kid's jacket pockets, pulling out two cans of Coke and a jumbo bag of Professor Kernel's Taffy-Covered Taco Balls.

Suddenly the kid had a jackknife out and he was holding it high.

"Get away, sucker. I'll whittle your face," he sneered.

Gabe nodded. "Yeah, well, everybody needs a hobby but—"

Gabe tossed the cans of pop at the kid and impaled the jumbo bag of Professor Kernel's Taffy-Covered Taco Balls on the blade, taking away the kid's edge. Gabe picked him up by the lapels of his jacket and slammed him back on the wide cover of the ice-cream freezer. The knife fell to the floor. Gabe put his face close to the kid's and gave him Jimmy Cagney.

"Oookay, mistah, I don't ever wanna see your ugly puss around here again or it's gonna be Swiss-cheese time. *Comprende?*"

The kid nodded, still sneering. Gabe shoved him to the door.

"Now, giddada here, punk."

Gabe kicked the jackknife out after him and laughed.

Nearing a half hour later, Gabe was filling a bag for a robin's-egg-blue-haired lady when the kid came back. He had the knife. He also had something else, which he was swinging around in his other hand. It was a bicycle chain.

"Hey hey, dirtball! I really liked your bike. Too bad. Too bad, punk!" He whipped the chain around one last time and let it fly at Gabe. Gabe ducked and took off after the kid, who was already outside. He was halfway down the block when Gabe came charging out. He looked down at his ten-speed. The tires were slashed all the way around.

"You little crud!" Gabe screeched. He started after the kid but it was too late. A successful capture was out of the question.

"Death! Death!" Gabe howled, making the thumbs-down gesture. "You hear, you little crudzoid! Death! Death! Death for you—"

Gabe suddenly realized there were people on the street, staring. Some were frowning; others were tittering to themselves. Gabe went back inside the store. The blue-haired lady had already left. With a free bag of groceries.

"Well, hell."

Ten after four, Gabe was perched precariously on the stool, chewing thoughtfully on a Milky Way, watching a very blow-dried, health-club couple cruise up and down the aisles. The phone jangled. Gabe scooped it up with his middle finger.

23

"Y'ello, Speller Groceteria," he said with a tune.

"Hi, Gabe. Jim here."

"Hey, guy."

"Hey. Just wanted to make sure you're comin' to the concert tonight."

"This is true. Wouldn't miss Pumpkin for the woild. Uh, can you pick me up here?"

"Can do. Why?"

"Some little maniac with a Swiss knife decided to play open-tire surgery on my poor *bicyclette.*"

"Tough stuff. Five?"

"On the nose."

"See you."

"Sayonara, son."

Coming up fast on five o'clock, Gabe was replenishing the long cigarette rack behind the counter. He didn't hear the back door open and close. He didn't hear the figure move slowly up the middle aisle. And he didn't hear the figure slip around the counter and come up behind him, arms outstretched.

Packs of Colts and Virginia Slims soared through the air as the hands seized him just below the ribs. Gabe spun around and landed on the high stool, nearly tipping over backward. His eyes rolled and he moaned when he saw who it was. Angela.

She was wearing a loving pair of white Jordache jeans and an equally affectionate rayon top with diagonal slashes of black and pink across it. The small v of her neckline changed into a capital letter as she leaned down toward Gabe, her arms on either side of him. She was only sixteen, but by her fourteenth year she had

24

acquired the anatomy of a woman. And she had used it to her advantage and amusement ever since.

"A little jumpy, Gabe?" she asked, grinning.

"Not till now."

She was nibbling on the head of a frosted gingerbread man. A crumb stuck in the corner of her mouth. She ran a red tongue across her thick lips, removing the bit of cookie. Her black, shimmering hair hung straight down, almost reaching Gabe's lap.

"I had a dream about you last night," she breathed into his face.

"No guff."

"Actually, it was more of a fantasy."

"Okay."

"It was so fantastically beautiful. Want me to tell you about it?"

"Nah, I'll take your word for it."

She forged an injured look. Then Gabe felt the fingers of her right hand close around his left thigh. A starfish of heat radiated from her grip. He wanted to tell her to take her hand away, but it couldn't be done. Staring into his eyes, Angela delicately bit off the gingerbread man's legs and held them between her front teeth, as if expecting Gabe to take a limb. He declined. With a tiny sigh, she let the cookie legs fall into her mouth.

"Gabe, why don't you ever ask me out?" she asked bashfully. Another forged emotion.

"Angie, listen—"

"Ohhh, I love it when you call me Angie."

"Angela, listen, I don't ask you out, basically, because you're already going out with two guys and one of them looks like Arnie Schwarzenegger's big bro—"

Before he had finished his sentence she had begun to run her fingernails lightly down his leg. Gabe stifled a giggle that popped up into his throat.

"You're not scared . . . are you, Gabe?"

"No, not at all. It's just that I'd like to keep my kneecaps on the front of my legs. I'm funny that way."

Just then, Gabe saw Jimmy's cream Mustang pull up in front. The horn sounded.

"Woop! Gotta go," Gabe said. He jumped up, grabbed his jacket, and squeezed past Angela.

"See you later," she said.

"Whether I'm there or not, eh?" Gabe said with a quick smile.

Outside, blue twilight was drooping into the city. Gabe picked up what remained of his bicycle and went over to the passenger window.

"Hey, howarya," Gabe asked.

"Heavily sedated. It's open."

Gabe stuffed the bike into the trunk, tossing the chain in with it, then came back around, and got in. Billy Idol was wailing from the backseat speakers. Jimmy was a gaunt, fair-skinned eighteen-year-old who looked like he belonged forever on some warm seashore instead of in some cold city. He was drinking a bottle of potent liquid in an extremely subtle brown paper bag, which he passed to Gabe. Gabe accepted the bottle, but he really didn't feel like getting swizzled tonight. He just felt like curling up and going to sleep. He chugalugged a substantial bolt, wondering just what he was drinking.

26

Whatever it was, it tasted like three hundred proof. Eyes tearing, he handed it back.

"N-no-hhhachk-no, thanks," he rasped. "Never touch the stuff."

TWO

Gabe and the small group he was with reached the auditorium twenty minutes before the scheduled start of the concert. Holloway's was alive and kicking with young life.

The group moved across the parking lot, which was black and sparkling from an early evening rain. Besides Gabe, there were four in the group. Jimmy Kemps, the proud owner of the Mustang that got them there. Sandra Murphy, a round-faced chesty lass who was a hopeless giggler. She was Jimmy's girl. Lee Banza, an animated youth who was part Korean and part Hawaiian, but was convinced he was a full-blooded Japanese. And told everyone so. And finally Samuel Niles, a quiet, long-haired boy who nobody knew much about.

Gabe didn't make it a steady practice to pal around with these people, but he had wanted to hear this concert for a long time. He didn't really pal around with anybody that much. In truth he couldn't say that he had any genuine friends in school. Just mates—no more no less.

The day was done. The sky had taken on an obsidian quality.

"It's friggin' cold!" Sandra whined as she pulled Jimmy's long arm further around her.

"Nipple erectus," Lee grunted, and lashed out with a dropkick in the gelid air. It was his effort to keep warm.

Sandra watched him and giggled. She glanced over at Samuel, who was looking away from the group.

"Sammy boy! Still with us?"

"Yeh."

"Sure, sure, Sammy," Lee muttered. He slipped a Camel between his lips and lit up. "It's a known fact you've been living in the ozone for the past year."

Sandra giggled. Samuel just smiled.

Gabe turned to Lee.

"Hey, you find employment yet?"

"Y'betcha. Medallion Steak House. I'm the headwaiter."

"Riiight. Let's get real here, man," Jimmy said.

"Your disbelief falls on deaf ears, James," Lee said haughtily. "I'll have you know I've worked my way up from the ranks of one."

"Kicking and clawing all the way," Gabe said.

"Yeah, and Mitzi is working there as one of the waitresses," Lee said importantly.

"Who?" Gabe asked.

"Mitzi Howse. Uhhh, she's in your I.A. class, Jim. Tall chick, blond hair down to her ankles. Yummy-yum-yummm."

"Oh, yeah," Jimmy acknowledged, nodding. "Nice girl. If you're into gargling Windex."

"What're you babbling about?" Lee asked.

"She's an English export, man. Positively punk all the way," Jimmy said.

"New Romantic," Lee said.

29

"Hardly," Jimmy said, laughing.

"You're the only waiter there?" Gabe asked.

"Yup. It just opened and the old guy who owns it wanted mostly waitresses, but he was looking for a waiter, too. And my dear old grandmama just happens to know the ancient dude, and so . . ."

"Hey, how *is* your grandma doing, Lee?" Gabe asked. "Still in the hospital or what?"

Lee flicked a live ash. Gabe watched it plummet and die.

"Well, Gabe, to put it bluntly, let's just say the old biddy has got one foot in the grave and the other one on a banana peel. In other words, she's—"

"—slipping, yes," Gabe finished it, nodding.

Sandra giggled. Gabe didn't find it so funny. Lee glanced at Gabe.

"You know, you really look dead, Gabe. Like we're talking George Romero time."

"You know, I really feel dead, thank you, *momma-san.*"

Sandra giggled. Jimmy turned to Lee over Sandra's head.

"Hey, Lee. You see that new pooch? I think she's in your science class. Anna something. Alpo city or what?"

"For sure. Was she born, or did they have to drill for her?"

Sandra giggled. Lee kept talking.

"Oh, man, you shoulda seen. She was drinkin' this milk by the lockers and I guess it went down the wrong way and she started to choke and yucka wotta mess. She looked just like . . . like Cujo right before they shot him!"

30

Sandra almost expired right there, laughing hysterically.

Reaching the entranceway, Gabe and Lee stood on either side, like high-society doormen. Clicking their heels, they made sweeping gestures with their arms. Jimmy and Sandra curtsied and went through. Samuel just smiled and followed.

Inside, the atmosphere changed immediately. The house was packed. Electric tension had turned the air warm and sticky. Nobody seemed to be able to stand still. The place was bumping, lifting, jumping movement.

As they pushed their way through the jungle of sweating bodies, Gabe heard Lee say "shirts" and saw him take off to the right.

Gabe did his best to stay with his small cluster, but in the frenzy of movement he lost them. He saw Samuel's long hair disappear into the throng.

Dark gray aisles were choked with people coming and going. Uniformed guards were all over, watching. A commotion ahead to the left caught Gabe's eye. Two large Chicano males were being shoved up against a wall. Gabe watched as they were spread-eagled and searched. One was swearing steadily; the other was crying.

The air blurred with smoke. Several huge pumpkin-shaped balloons bounced from one person to another. Enormous orange and black banners with "Tissue Blade Tour '84" blazoned across them hung from the ceiling directly above the high stage. Steel pumpkins atop the band's massive amplifiers vibrated as if in anticipation. Colored lights attached to the

31

edge of the stage glowed. Overhead even more lights burned brightly, illuminating the polished instruments.

Squinting, Gabe thought he could see small cages on either side of the platform, but he wasn't sure. Looking for a place to stand, he made his way through the buzzing crowd. From out of nowhere he was grabbed hard by his left arm. He turned to see a leather boy. His hair was bleached orange and his face was snow-white, given color only by the cosmetics he wore. The eyes were a vapid water-blue, heavily lined with mascara. Lavender rouge slashed down his cheeks to the apple-red lipstick that glistened on his mouth. He had a delicate gold ring in his left nostril. He almost looked pretty.

"You have some with you?" His voice was a reedy whisper, but he was close enough so that Gabe could hear what he said. "Right?"

Gabe shook his head.

"Uhhh, no, man. I'm all cleaned out."

The leather boy's grip was so tight that his hand almost circled Gabe's arm.

"Hey, I need some now. Just a bit. Just one hit. C'mon, c'mon."

Gabe jerked his arm loose.

"I said no. 'Kay?"

Gabe started to shoulder his way past the boy. Then he saw it—the glint of a blade. A scalpel, of all things. Gabe's face went chalky. He could not believe this was happening to him twice in one day. Suddenly he felt a need for a jumbo bag of Professor Kernel's Taffy-Covered Taco Balls.

The leather boy held the long-bladed scalpel low, pointing at Gabe's intestines. Gabe put his hands up in front of him, palms out.

"Hey, whoa, c'mon, buddy. Take it easy, m'man," Gabe coaxed. "C'mon, just mellow out. I really don't—"

"Slug!" the boy hissed viciously. The muscles of his face tightened, contorted. He wasn't pretty anymore. Gabe could see that there would be no more talking with the guy. In fact, it began to dawn on Gabe that he could very well be looking into the eyes of a psychopath. He began to put some space between them, moving backward. Licking his thin lips, the boy with murder in his long fingers moved on Gabe. Then a whooping, laughing throng of adolescents crushed in, filling the space to form a writhing barrier between them. Gabe pivoted and ran through a dense curtain of people, swiftly weaving his way through the crowd.

Gasping, he made his way over to the far wall and found a space beside a slender girl with frizzy blond hair. She was leaning back against the cool concrete wall, her hands tucked behind her. She stared blankly ahead into bodies. She wore an old Journey Tour '81 jersey, which hung loosely out of blue jeans that hugged her like another layer of flesh. Looking closer, Gabe recognized her as a girl who had been in his art class, but he couldn't recall her name.

"Hiya," he offered.

No response. He wiped his sweating face with his jacket sleeve.

"Uh, 'member me? Gabe Holden. Musko's art class last year?"

Nothing.

"Well . . . this concert should be pretty awesome. Better be, for the bills we had to put out, eh? Crud! You shoulda seen what happened to me over there. I was just—"

She turned and looked up at him. Success! Gabe thought.

"I'm going now," she said, pushed herself off the wall, and melted away into the mob.

"Yeah, great. Knock yourself out." Gabe sighed, leaned back against the wall, and tucked his hands behind him.

Then she was there, filling in the space the blond had left behind. Her skin was cinnamon and sprinkled lightly with freckles. Her lico-rice-black hair reached down just past her shoulder blades, feathered beads hanging from it. She had big chocolate eyes that were not to be believed. Her plump strawberry lips seemed to have a permanent smirk on them. But the girl, herself, didn't look too happy at the moment.

Her clothing was simple, trim, and as spot-lessly white as vanilla ice cream. She had on tennis shoes, rugby pants, and a jacket with the collar turned up. A thin gold chain hung around her throat.

She's gotta be somebody's baby, Gabe moaned inside. Oh, yeah, no question about it, boys. Any second now, ol' super-stud is going to come crashing through the crowd and swat me out of the way.

Gabe waited. Nothing.

"Hullo," he ventured.

She turned and looked up at him from under her bangs.

"Hi."

"Having fun?" he asked.

"Oh, fer sure. Outstanding. Just . . . out-standing."

"You like Pumpkin?" Gabe asked.

"That's why I'm here."

Gabe nodded. "Here with friends?" he asked.

"Was. I kind of got left behind. Sob, sob."

"No great loss?"

"No great loss."

She looked away, then back at Gabe.

"You too?" she asked.

"Me too."

"No great loss?"

"Well, it's nice to be here with someone you know, you know?"

"Yeah."

Gabe looked around. No sign of super-stud.

"Um . . . I'm Gabe."

"Kate."

Gabe nodded again.

"You still in school?" he asked.

"Yep. T. Gales High."

"Oh, yeah. Nice school."

"If you like schools."

"Not especially."

Pause.

"So, what do you do?" Gabe asked.

"Go to school."

"Other than that."

"Work in my father's record store."

"Oh, yeah?"

"Oh, yeah."

Long pause.

"You still in school?" she asked. The smirk on her lips had stretched into a smile of curiosity.

"Yep. J. L. Lloyd High."

"Oh, yeah. Nice school."

"If you like schools."

"Not especially."

Pause. They swapped smiles.

"So, what do *you* do?" Kate asked.

"Go to school," they said together, laughing.

"Other than that," she said.

"I'm a Habnin salesman."

"Habnin? What's Habnin?"

"Nothin' much. What's happenin' with you?"

She groaned and closed her eyes, nodding. The ice had been crushed.

"No, really," she said.

"You really want to know?"

"I really want to know."

"I make dragons."

" 'Scuse me?"

Gabe grinned.

The lights above the spacious hall flickered and dimmed, and the noise level rose to a roar. A series of rapid-fire bursts of colored smoke came from the front of the stage. A group of silhouetted bodies ran across the stage and took their positions. Without warning, an enormous sheet of electric blue light erupted from the rear of the platform and reached for the ceiling of the auditorium.

Then a pair of hunched figures on either side of the stage went over to the cages. In a spectacular flourish, clouds of sparrows flew upward across the luminous sheet of light and turned into glittering silhouettes. Dazzling. The dark birds headed for the open windows near the ceiling. A few stayed on the ledges.

Gabe felt a chill race up, down, and up his spine.

Then the opening bars of the old favorite, "Razor Birds," worked their way through the multitude. Cheering went up from thousands of voices. Lighters were ignited.

Pumpkin-X was there.

Soon the opening bars became a simmering volcano that had no choice but to explode. Gabe felt his eyes begin to water and the teeth in his head start to vibrate with the sheer force of it. Numbing.

The well-known song shattered in conclusion. The listeners screamed their appreciation and cried out requests. Without a break, the charismatic lead singer, Tick, jerked the band into "Bloody Ribbons." Radiant bursts of light darted back and forth around the edge of the stage. Gasps whisked through the masses and the cheers mounted.

The potent spell was cast. The transformation had taken place. The youths. They were all someone—something—else now. An unstoppable force of a wild nature. An energy that had been bottled up for so very long was now, at long last, uncorked. It could not be explained or understood.

The song escalated to a falsetto blast and ended. The lights blinked out and a long, incandescent yellow beam fell on Tick. Now alone in a solo, knees bent, back arched, he worked the chords of "Hallway Trips." With his fingers curved like the claws of some great feline, he seemed determined to rip the metal strings right off of his electric guitar. The instrument wailed in pain.

It was at that moment that Gabe realized that Tick did not need the group behind him. He could dominate the audience alone. He was the warrior chieftain, and his guitar was his glistening two-edged sword.

The drummer soon slammed in with a hefty jungle beat on his tom-toms. Then the keyboardist joined with a steady pattern of shimmering bullets of sound that turned the song into an urgent message. The entire band was well into it now. The music swelled like a screaming cyclone that ripped and tore through the fog-like haze.

The crowd was howling like dogs waiting to be fed, pushing and shoving each other onward. The steel pumpkins atop the huge thundering speakers were now blazing as if reflecting the crowd's fury. The music was an unending tidal wave of sound, pouring and pouring raw power over the spectators.

Somebody in studded black leather lunged for the stage, scrambling up onto it. Tick kicked him in the head, knocking him back into the audience.

Glaring into the sea of blooming life, Tick's painted face broke into a grin. A pitiless grin.

York's grin, Gabe thought, frowning. *That's York's grin.* Almost exactly the same. Top front lip curled back, nostrils flared at an angle. Almost like all the dragons' grins.

Pondering this, Gabe saw something pop up from the crowd, fly in his direction, and disappear a few feet away. He saw a small white flash accompanied by an explosion that joggled his innards.

People toppled like chess pieces before Gabe's eyes. He staggered back, arms wheeling in a futile effort to keep his balance. He sucked in fumes and opened his mouth, gagging, breathing fire. His head bounced off something hard. The wall. A Roman candle went off behind his eyes leaving a torrent of blinding sparkles. He could hear his name. Gabe. Gabe. Ga . . .

He felt his knees begin to slide inside his jeans and point toward the floor.

(Dear God . . . my head . . . it's come open. . .)

Everything spun by and he was gone, but not before he thought he could see the leather boy coming for him through the crowd. . . .but the boy now had the face . . . the face of an old woman . . . and had the eyes . . . the eyes of a cat. . . .

Agonizing blotches of light. On/off. On/off. On/off.

Gabe was in a blazing whirlpool. His head was being consumed by white fire. The fire had tasted his brain, found it good, and begun to dine.

He heard music. Blue Oyster Cult. He sniffed. Perfume. Lemon. He opened his eyes halfway. Streetlights flashed by. He focused. Kate's face filled the picture.

"Hiya." She spoke lightly.

Gabe was laid out in the back seat of Jimmy's car. His head was in Kate's lap and his feet were in Samuel's. Jimmy and Lee were in the front seat arguing. Gabe couldn't hear what it was about over the music. Sandra was between them, her head thrown back, her wavy brown hair dangling over the seat.

Gabe watched the streetlights flash by overhead.

(This is unreal. Dream-like. Except in dreams you don't hurt like this.)

Kate's window was partially open. Gabe watched a thin strand of her hair blow across her mouth. Gabe sucked in the cold air and moistened his numb lips.

"My . . . head," he croaked.

"Does it hurt?" she asked.

"My . . . head."

"Does it hurt, Gabe?"

"My . . . head."

"You said that. Does it hurt much?"

Gabe tried to sit up. Cauterizing pain. He nearly blacked out.

"Yes. It hurts much."

"We thought you were dead."

"I am. Mourners please omit flowers."

Lee and Sandra twisted around. They were drinking Budweiser and both of them were slightly blitzed.

"Hey, buddy. How're ya doin'?" Lee asked. "How's the head feel?"

"Crunchy Granola," Gabe answered.

"Uh-huh."

Gabe attempted to sit up again. The fire surged through the tunnels in his brain. He stopped and rested his head between Kate's breasts. Lee raised his eyebrows. Kate smiled. Sandra giggled. Gabe gave a weak "ha-ha" and dropped back into her lap.

"Everybody? Kate. Kate? Everybody."

"We already met," Jimmy spoke into the rearview mirror. "You're half an hour late with the intros, Gabe."

"Half an hour? 'Sthat how long I been out?"

" 'Bout that," Lee said. "Want a swallow?"

He held the can out to Gabe. Gabe took it. It wasn't very cool.

"Don't spill any, eh?" Jimmy said seriously, turning his head toward the back seat. The Mustang veered over to the other side of the street, heading for an oncoming camper.

"Hey, front and center, *amigo*," Lee said, reaching around Sandra to jab Jimmy's shoulder. Jimmy got back to his side.

"Pulls a little, huh?" Lee asked.

"A little," Jimmy said.

Gabe tilted his head up and looked at Kate.

"Wait a minute. What're you doing here? Did your good buddies leave without you?"

"Well, they were sort of every-man-for-yourself buddies. If you get back to the car in time, you get a ride home. And I couldn't very well just leave you lying there in a pile, could I?"

"Very admirable, dear. What exactly happened, anyway? We're listening to Pumpkin, then ka-flooey!"

"We're not sure."

"Yo, guys? What happened?" Gabe asked the front seat, giving the beer back to Lee.

"Aaahh, some total brainstem tossed some kinda bomb onto your side of the floor," Lee said. "Pretty sorry scene. Gave new meaning to the word 'pandemonium.'"

"Yeah, everybody was just goin' rank," Jimmy said, turning around. "Piggies were really stomping heads. Pumpkin got the hell outa there. Except Tick, that crazy freak. He threw his strings into the crowd and just stood there, screaming at them to come up. They nearly killed the sucker."

"Anyway, Kate there found you first, completely out of it, then I found her, then every-body found us, and we all hauled ass. Yours," Lee said, ripping open another beer.

Gabe nodded painfully. The music from the front banged around inside his skull.

"Hey, Jim, can you turn the thing down a notch?"

"Yeah."

BOC died.

Clenching his teeth, Gabe pushed himself up and sat back between Kate and quiet Samuel. The fire in his head narrowed into searing flames behind his eyes. He felt around at the back of his skull. It was extremely tender but there was no blood. Just some grit.

"Blood?" Kate asked.

"Blood! Oh, man, did you get it on the seat?" Jimmy asked, turning all the way around. He looked as if he was verging on tears.

"No, no. Hush, hush now, chile. Your motor car is allll safe. Momma's takin' care of every-thin', now," Gabe said.

"Hey, bub! This is my ivory chariot," Jimmy said, looking gravely at Gabe. "It is without blemish, scratch, dent, or zit inside and out."

B-PPHHHAAAAAAAAAAAAAAAAAAA!!!

The brilliant glare of a transport truck's headlights froze their faces, and the blaring horn took hold of their brains in a fist of noise. Gabe, Kate, Sandra, and Lee all screamed in harmony. Jimmy was beyond screaming. Samuel just opened his eyes a little wider than usual.

In one convulsive jerk, Jimmy wrenched the steering wheel to his right, tacking the Mustang back to the correct lane, missing the truck by shuddering inches.

Gabe lost his balance and his head collided with Kate's window. It wasn't the thing to do. The pain was beyond imagination. He gripped his skull between his hands as a shriek oozed its way out between his teeth. There was a fierce compression on his brain, a drastic increase of pressure. It felt like that rosy bowl of soaking Jell-O up there was caught between the blistering teeth of a nutcracker that was squeezing and squeezing and squeeeeeeeeAAAAA-*AAA*. . . .

(. . . c-can't take this . . . anymo—)

. . . it stopped. Tears formed at the corners of his eyes.

It had felt, to Gabe, as if something up there actually shifted and . . . broke.

Suddenly he felt very sick and a little frightened. The whole automobile seemed to give one big fluttering sigh.

"Oh, kids. Oooohh, kids," Lee exhaled, sliding down in his seat.

"Oh, God, that—that was so close, so close. . . ." Sandra murmured.

Blinking rapidly, Gabe pushed back his hair and looked at Kate. She mirrored his expression: wide eyes, rapid blinking. Gabe gave a quick giggle through the pulsing pain.

"My, my, yes, that *was* close. Would you say that was close, Gabe?" Lee asked, fidgeting.

"Yes, I'd say that was close," Gabe muttered, holding his head.

"Just what I thought. Close. Would you say that was close, Sammy?"

"Close."

"Real close."

"Very close."

"Very, *very* close."

"Okay," Lee said. "All those who thought that was close say 'aye.' "

"Aye."

"Aye."

"Aye."

"Aye."

"Aye."

Slowing the car down to a stroll, Jimmy detached his right hand from the steering wheel and held it in the air.

"All right. Sorry, people. Apologies all around, okay? Okay? Everybody?"

Sandra got up on her knees and cuffed his head.

"You—you twitty person!" she screamed hoarsely. "I am not impressed!"

"That's telling him, Sandy. Give 'im the works," Gabe said.

"Hey, Jim, buddy. I hear there's some really excellent career opportunities over in Lebanon right about now. Want me to sign you up?" Lee asked. He wasn't laughing.

"I said I'm sorry."

"I've got a good idea," Gabe said, massaging the side of his head. "Why don't we just paste a sticker on his butt. 'Warning: The surgeon general has determined that Jimmy Kemps is extremely dangerous to your . . .' "

"I *said* I'm sorry."

"Y'okay, okay, man," Lee said, popping open another brew.

A long thick silence followed. Jimmy turned on the radio. Asia. Lee smoked and drank. Sandra fell asleep. Samuel said nothing. Gabe felt sick.

"Fun evening," Kate said.

"Yeah, well, here's where the action is," Gabe said.

"That's for sure."

"So. Do we know each other?" Gabe asked.

"Think so. We were talking when Pumpkin came on, and I thought you were saying that you make dragons. Stupid, yes, I know, but—"

"I do."

"What?"

"Hey, what do you wanna do, Gabe?" Jimmy asked, turning his head halfway. "We were kind of heading for a clinic or—"

"Uh, no, no, forget that. Just drop me off at home base. I'll survive."

Jimmy turned a corner sharply. Gabe's head started to spin to the left, then reversed direction. He couldn't tell what area of the city they were in. Buildings, cars, signs were all out of focus, surreal. Kate looked into his face.

"You sure you're okay?"

Gabe smiled.

"Just jake. A couple of aspirin and a shower and I'm laughin'."

Lee threw back his head, killing the rest of the beer, and chucked the can out of the car window. Gabe watched it bounce away into the night. Suddenly a sickly warmth spread over him and filled the car. Quickly realizing he was about to be violently ill, he pushed himself up to the front.

"Uh, Jim? I think you better pull over, man. And I'm talking right now."

Jimmy turned the radio down a bit.

"Huh?"

"I said I think you better—"

"Whoa, Gabriel," Lee said, "you're not exactly the picture postcard of health, son. You want another Bud?" he asked, coming off sounding like some Monday night football commercial.

Gabe inhaled the smell of beer mixed with cigarette off of Lee's breath. Regretfully.

"No, I don't. I just think Jim better pull—"

"Gabe, are you okay?" Kate asked, touching his shoulder.

Gabe gritted his teeth.

"No, I'm not. Jim, I think you really oughta—"

"Hey, Lee, get him another can," Jim said.

"He said he didn't want one, and watch the road, will ya?" Lee said. "Remember the road? Long black thing with—"

"Don't start it, man," Jimmy warned.

He turned another giddy corner.

"You don't want another beer, Gabe?" Jimmy asked.

Gabe gripped Jimmy's shoulder. He was losing it.

"No. Just pull ov—"

"Of course he doesn't want another beer," Sandra said, waking up. "It'd probably make him barf."

"Well, sweetums, how're we supposed to know?" Jimmy asked.

He steered mercilessly around another corner. Gabe was reaching for the blond-haired boy's throat.

"Jim . . ."

"Hey, ain't there supposed to be something in

beer that helps the stomach when it's sick?" Lee asked, frowning.

"Jim, I'm gonna . . . urp!"

"No, no. That's wine. Wine helps the stomach. It's in the Bible, somewhere," Jimmy said.

"Jim!"

Samuel sat up and tapped Jimmy on the shoulder.

"What?"

"Gabe is going to woof his groceries all over your precious ivory chariot in, judging from his face, about one second," he said offhandedly, and sat back.

Jimmy twisted around and looked at Gabe.

Screaming like a maniac and driving just like one, Jimmy jerked the Mustang over to the shoulder of the road. Gabe sailed over Kate and was out of the car before it came to a fishtailing stop. He let go in a ditch. Shaking, he walked back up to the puttering car. Raising his face to the sky, he swallowed a deep purifying drink of night air and climbed in.

"Home, James . . . home," Gabe said.

Three

The Mustang glided over to the sidewalk in front of the house. The guttural drumming of the engine was the only sound on the dark street. The right back door opened and Gabe got out, his jacket hanging over his shoulder. He bent down on one knee to Kate.

"Um, so. Can I see you again sometime?" he asked in a low voice.

"Originality at its very best," Lee said from the front.

"Do you mind very much? We're just doing a little mumbling here," Gabe said.

"Why don't you hustle your buns on down to the store?" Kate asked.

"Name."

"Soaring Records. Second floor in the Q-Dome."

"Q-Dome Mall? Hey, my sister works there, on the bottom floor."

"Oh, yeah?"

"Oh, yeah. So. I'll catch ya on the flip side."

"Saturday," she said.

"Saturday," Gabe repeated.

"After work."

"After work."

"Five-thirty."

"Five-thirty."

"Be there—"

"—or be square."

"Damn straight."

"Yes'm."

She gave a little smirk. Gabe looked up and saw that everybody was staring at him with big cheesy grins on their faces.

"Nighty night, peoples," Gabe said.

"Nighty night, Gabe," they all chimed sweetly.

He slammed the door and lifted his bike and chain out of the trunk. He stood there and watched as the car turned the corner at the north end of the street and drove out of sight.

Gabe's head ached terribly. A flame flicked behind his left eye. His free hand went to it and pressed hard. He walked his deflated ten-speed up to his house and parked it beside the front door. The porch light wasn't on, but he could see a brightness through the curtains drawn across the large bay window. Deciding not to tell his parents anything, he opened the front door and went in.

The television was on. Mom and his little brother, Tyler, were curled up on the love seat. Dad was all but lost to view, sitting back in his deep rocker-recliner. The glow from the twenty-six-inch screen bathed their faces almost lovingly. When they turned away to look at Gabe, the light cut them in half. Looking closer, Gabe saw all three of them were wearing 3-D glasses. He had to laugh.

"Very punk, guys," he said, smiling.

"Hi. You're home early," Dad said, taking off his plastic and paper shades.

"Fast songs," Gabe replied.

"Have a good time?" Mom asked. She kept her glasses on.

"Blew me away. Do we have any aspirin?"

"Ummm, there should be a few left in a bottle on top of the bread box," Mom said.

Leaning on the back of the sofa that divided the foyer and the living room, Gabe untied his Nikes. The rest of the family's shoes were loosely lined up, black mouths gaping, tongues out, as if waiting for some tasty morsel of meat. He squinted to see what they were watching. Two red pinheads gleamed on the VCR that sat on top of the television console.

"What's on?" Gabe asked.

"Creature from the Black Lagoon," Tyler said, his eyes not moving from the screen. He was munching from a large wooden bowl of popcorn glittering with melted butter.

"Mm. On top of the bread box, Mom?"

"What?"

"Aspirin."

"Oh, yes."

After downing three of the little white tablets, Gabe trudged upstairs. His legs had strangely taken on weight. Reaching the top, he heard his older sister, Rachel, in the shower. He banged on the bathroom door.

"Hey! Y'all be in there long?" he called over the sound of spraying water.

"Bugger off!" she yelled back.

"Thank you!"

Deciding to skip on the shower, Gabe headed for bed. His head was an oven. Pulling off his sweaty clothes he suddenly realized something.

(Concussion . . . what if I have a concussion?

50

. . . Can't go to sleep . . . gotta stay awake . . . all friggin' night . . . shower.)

Waiting until Rachel was finished, Gabe heard the bathroom door open and her bedroom door close. He grabbed his worn and sagging black terrycloth robe and ambled over to the bathroom. Seeing the glow from the TV screen downstairs, Gabe heard Tyler's excited voice.

" 'Kay! 'Kay! Good part's coming up here. Just wait a sec!" On the screen, the Creature from the Black Lagoon swam up and out of its gloomy lair and made for the surface.

Gabe closed the bathroom door behind him.

And it began.

He stuffed his clothes into the wicker hamper and knelt beside the sea-green bathtub. He twisted the taps hoping there was some hot water left after Rachel's shower. There was. He stepped in and warm taffy-like water gushed down over him. It felt absolutely delicious on his naked body. He turned the hot water spigot until it was just right and picked up a white waxy cake of soap. He rubbed it unhurriedly between his hands and lathered his arms, chest, stomach, legs, and feet. He left the soap on and reached up for the Johnson's Baby Shampoo, the family shampoo, on a yellow plastic shelf beside the Water Pik. He poured the thick golden liquid into his left palm and kneaded it into his hair. It foamed down his neck onto his chest.

Downstairs, Tyler leaned forward on his knees, eyes intent.

"Tyler, you're going to get nightmares tonight," Mom warned.

"No chance, now ssshh."

The Creature from the Black Lagoon headed

toward the pink legs of the pretty swimmer treading water.

Gabe put his face into the rush of water and opened his mouth. He couldn't get enough of it. The heated water rinsed his hair and ran down his slippery skin. The pain in his head actually seemed to wash away with the soap. He twisted off the water. Quiet. Dripping, he opened the shower curtain, stepped out onto the fringed bath mat, and pulled the curtain closed again.

The Creature from the Black Lagoon reached out with a grotesque claw to seize the delicate ankle of the pretty swimmer.

The air in the bathroom had turned to a regular murky-white London fog from the shower steam. Pain forgotten, Gabe began to dry himself with a big orange towel. He worked the towel through his wet hair, across his neck and chest, then down to his—

P-AASSSSSSSSSHHH!

The pretty swimmer screamed.

The two fists exploded through the shower curtain on either side of Gabe. For a slice of a second Gabe saw green then blackness as the hands clamped onto his face from behind, like two huge spiders. Gabe clawed at the white air as he was jerked off his feet and backward. Metal rings screeched along metal pole as the curtain was ripped loose when Gabe and his attacker slammed into the bottom of the bathtub.

Legs kicking, arms jabbing, punching wildly, Gabe tried to execute some means of offense, defense, any-fense! But it was all wasted. He tried to scream but his attacker's fingers were stuffed in his mouth. He bit down hard, hoping for something, but received nothing. His thrashings started weakening when he felt two power-ful fingers spread into a Y and move up past his nose to his eyeballs and press inward.

In a frantic burst of energy, Gabe lodged his feet against the slick porcelain walls of the tub and pushed himself up. Incredibly, his attacker went up with him. Gabe threw his entire weight back and smashed himself and his assailant against the wall. He still could not break the hold on him. In a futile effort, Gabe brought his right fist back, hoping to hit his foe, but instead hit the wall. A knife of pain stabbed his hand and up his forearm. Then he heard the voice rambling through the curtain.

"Get out, Daddy. Get out and stay out."

The words sounded as if they had been run through molasses. Gabe struck back with his fist again, but this time he hit something else. The Water Pik. His fingers closed around the handle and he got the tool off its hook. He brought it forward and back in a fast stab. This time he hit flesh. He heard a yelp and felt his at-tacker's embrace loosen.

Gabe spun around, but before they came face to face his feet were easily kicked out from un-der him and he went down, taking the shower curtain, which was between them, with him. He crashed on his back with a resounding smack.

"It's not time yet."

Lying there, almost in a cocoon, Gabe heard the loud thumpity-thumps on the bathroom door.

"Gabriel! For the last time, are you all right? Gabe!" Mom.

Raymond, Marie, Rachel, and Tyler Holden were all standing in a rough semicircle around the entrance to the bathroom. The door whipped

53

open. Robe on, a very miffed Gabriel stamped into the hall. He was dragging a dripping Sid behind him.

"Funny stuff, Rachel. A real riot, you sadistic creep!" Gabe said, almost yelling.

"What're you talking about?" Rachel asked, frowning. She had her pea-green velour robe on.

"Gabriel—" Mom started.

"Gabe, just what are you talking about?" Dad asked.

"This rodent sneaked into the bathroom and openly and viciously assaulted my person. She nearly gouged out my eyeballs!" Gabe said loudly, pointing at a bewildered Rachel.

"What?" Mom exclaimed, looking at Rachel.

"What!" Rachel exclaimed, considerably louder.

"Snuck into the bathroom while I was in the shower. Funny, I never pictured you as the incestuous type, Rache," Gabe spat.

"Shut up, you little weirdo! I was in my room the whole time!" Rachel yelled at Gabe.

"Booger nuggets! And what's with this 'Get out, Daddy, get out' crap?"

"What?"

"You know what I'm talkin' about. You said that right before I got you with the Water Pik!"

"Are you on some kind of wild chemical, Gabe?" Rachel said, incredulous.

"Don't try to get out of it, Rachel. And look! Look what you did to Sid!" Gabe stood the creature on his feet. Water was running off his pebbled skin in trickling streams.

Tyler snickered. He was still wearing his 3-D glasses.

"Shut yer face, shrimpball, or I—"

"Okay, Gabe, that'll do for tonight," Dad said. "You slipped in the tub, but you can't blame Rachel for that. And what were you doing with Sid in there in the first place? That's your fault."

"No way! She put him in there! You're gonna pay, girl! Do you know how long it took me to—"

"Ohh, no, Gabe. You ripped the curtain right off!" Mom said from the bathroom.

"No, I didn't! This scuzzball crudhead did! I keep telling y—"

"Scuzzball crudhead! Okay, that's it, folks! I'm not taking this garbage from some snvu—" Rachel cut off and stormed into her room. "You are really warped in the head, you know that, Gabe?"

"Huh! You're the warped one, honey! More like depraved!"

"All right, now, that'll be e-nough!" Dad said sternly, holding up his hands like a traffic cop. "Let's put a hold on the name-calling for the day, shall we?"

Rachel banged her door shut.

"Rachel!" Dad called.

"Yessir, ladies and geraniums, there goes Miss Crunchy Crudola 1984," Gabe said, heading for his room.

"Gabe, I said no more," Dad warned.

Gabe closed his door and turned on the little shaded lamp with a plastic Ford Model A base sitting on his desk top. The small bulb outlined his cheekbones and lips in a tender light. He set the dragon down in the middle of his room, went over and flicked to RADIO on his immense silver-colored portable stereo radio/cassette recorder. Sammy Hagar's "Rise of the Animal" swelled from the speakers.

55

Gabe wrenched open his closet and pulled out an age-old Sears ironing board. He unfolded the screeching metal legs, clicked them into place, and set it up in the center of his room. After Mom had bought herself a new one, she had given this antique to Gabe for him to work on his early creations. It was her way of showing that she was honestly interested in what her son was doing. He smoothed the chartreuse padded cover and ran his palms over the rippling ginger-colored water stains that spiraled around the board. He hoisted Sid up onto it. The dragon's prodigious back took up the board, so that his four strapping limbs dangled over the sides. Then Gabe grabbed a clear plastic bag off his top closet shelf and dumped out the contents. Flannel rags, sponges, cleaning syrups, a collection of frazzled toothbrushes, and a litter of invaluable miscellanea. Mumbling disgustedly to himself, he began to dry Sid, running a flannel rag over the coarse pebbled hide of the dragon's hideous frame. Sid hadn't always been like this. None of the Dragons Three had. No, they had been very much different, once . . . upon a time.

Through the music, a scene from six weeks earlier came to Gabe. . . .

He was at the Tally-Ho Toys building, sitting in the stark office of the new creative director, a position one step below the president of the small company. Her name was Mrs. B. Valieri. The very first thing that Gabe noticed about her was her face. It was a cruel geometric face. High triangular cheekbones led directly to a flat jawline that darted back to her ears. She had sallow skin that was stretched tight like a sheet of wax around the carved bones of her face. The pale flesh was given color by a wealth of make-up. Paints of life. Her raven hair, silvered at the temples, was pulled back in a hamburger bun. She wore a loose slate-colored blouse with puffed sleeves. Around her neck hung a pearl necklace, with earrings to match. She was toppling over into her forties. Gabe found she bore a frightening resemblance to Cruella de Vil, the unfeeling villainess of *One Hundred and One Dalmatians.*

She jotted down a note, slipped it into a manila folder she had in front of her, put the folder into the top drawer of her aluminum desk, and pulled out another folder. She looked up and acknowledged Gabe's existence with a smile. A plastoid smile. The same one Gabe had "heard" on the phone.

"Gabriel."

"Mrs. Valieri."

She went back to the yawning folder and traced along a line with a silver pen.

"Mm, yes. Quite discouraging." She spoke lightly into the folder.

"Dis . . . couraging?" Gabe asked, shifting his numbed buttocks in his hard wooden chair.

She looked up as if he had vulgarly spoken out of turn.

"Yes, Mr. Conet's memo on you. He states that you are very young, which I now see you are."

"Why is that discouraging?"

Mrs. Valieri placed her elbows on her desk top and granted Gabe a half-smile. He could almost see the condescension dripping from her

57

lips. He decided then that he didn't much like this woman.

"Gabe, you are young, and young people make mistakes. Many mistakes."

She went back to the folder.

"But, according to Mr. Conet, while you have been here at Tally-Ho, you have shown yourself to be a dependable, agreeable, and inventive young man. A sound risk."

"Yeah, well, Malcolm likes his Johnnie Walker," Gabe said with a grin.

She looked up, eyes narrowing.

"I beg your pardon?" she asked slowly.

"I'm . . . kidding."

"Oh," she said with a small nod, and looked back down.

"You first came to Tally-Ho a little over two years ago with Marcus the Black Panther, Yin and Yang, the Gorilla Twins, and Makbeth the Scottish Bear. None of these really went anyplace."

"No, but Malcolm said he—"

She held up her silver pen and continued to read.

"Now you've designed the . . . Dragons Three?"

"Yeah, they're a set. Here."

Having brought York along, Gabe reached down and brought him up to his full height. The dragon cleared the desk top from his belly up. He had a bright red Shriner's fez and was wearing one of Gabe's suits that he had outgrown a year or so ago. He looked very dapper. Mrs. Valieri put her pen down.

"Very good. *Very* good. You made him big."

"Yeah, I always wanted to do that. It took me forever but I got it done. Uh, Mrs. Valieri? I had this idea, see. I was planning on making more of them, y'know? Kind of a series. Sort of like a *race* of dragons, each having its own name. Kinda following in the footy-prints of the Smurfs or the Care Bears or the Cabbage Patch Kids or—"

Mrs. Valieri raised her face to Gabe. Her eyeballs had turned into orbs of ice.

"I don't ever want to hear those *names* in this office again." The constrained words were broken pieces of crystal, slicing the air in the room. She reached across her desk and touched York's muzzle.

"Why did you put on all this green fake fur?" she asked, back to smiling.

"Uh, well, y'know, cuddly, safe for the kids."

She gave a quick nod.

"You made all three the same?"

"Basically. Um, Malcolm was thinking—"

She held up her index finger, staring at the dragon. "What're the electronics?"

"There aren't any."

"What? Why? We have all the equipment here, and every one of our freelancers has made his prototypes electric in one way or another. Why not you?"

"Well, y'see, toys are for kids. And kids have humongous imaginations, every one of 'em. So, I decided a while ago that when I made my creations I would leave the motions of them entirely up to the 'theater of their minds.' See, I made all three dragons with sort of an Erector Set skeleton surrounded by a thick foam. The skeleton is made out of a hard fiberglass tubing with hinges so the head can turn and the back and knees can bend. Same with the tail. And see, the hands can grip."

Gabe clicked the thumb and three fat fingers into a fist. He looked just like a little boy showing off a new toy.

"Malcolm went along with this when he was here," Gabe said, "but he did talk me into putting in these—what I call 'Christmas lights'— for eyes."

He flicked a tiny white switch at the base of York's head. The cheerful eyes went on, an intense, glowing amber. Gabe turned them off.

"It's light now, but at night they look pretty good," Gabe said.

She leveled her blue, feline eyes at him.

"What do you mean by 'good'?" she asked seriously.

"Well, uh, scary, spooky, they glow in the dark, y'know."

She slapped her hand on the desk top. "Exactly," she said, almost in a whisper. Her plastic smile elongated as she put her hands together, interlacing the bony fingers.

Gabe scratched at the back of his head, a trifle perplexed.

"What exactly do you mean by 'exactly'?"

"Changes," the woman sputtered.

"Changes," Gabe echoed.

"Big changes."

"Big changes."

"Tally-Ho is about to take its leave of the red."

"It is."

"Yes. Out of the red and into black. Deep into black. It's *time* for Tally-Ho. And do you know how?"

Gabe gave a little shake of his head.

"Aggression, that's how. We're going to have it in everything we do here at Tally-Ho Toys.

And that means a brand-new look to every one of Tally-Ho's models, from here on out." She picked up her pen and withdrew a bit into her high-backed black leather chair. Gabe's eyebrows creased.

"New look?" he asked cautiously.

"Hostile." She showed teeth.

Gabe arched one eyebrow. She started to flick her pen back and forth in the air so fast it became a silver blur.

"From the tame to the savage. From the domesticated to the bestial. The subdued to the rapacious. From the submissive . . . to the enraged!"

(Somebody, anybody, get the cookie truck up here, pronto! Geez!)

"Uh, lemme see if I got this," Gabe said, moving up to the edge of his chair. "From now on, you want to make all the stuffed critters and what-have-you that come through Tally-Ho, uh, you want to make sure that they're, well . . . mean?"

"Merciless," she emphasized brightly.

"Right. And you wanna start with my dragons."

"Not quite, Gabe. While we're talking there are two other models in the works. But now, *yours,* well. Your Dragons Three are *ideal* for this project. I think they just might be the springboard we're going to need. My friend, we are about to usher in a distinct new line of stuffed animals. What do you say?"

Gabe rubbed a finger along the bridge of his nose.

"Well, Mrs. Valieri, I tell ya, when Malcolm was boss, he told me about this other toy company, about the size of this one, and they had

61

tried, uh, something like what you're talking about."

Mrs. Valieri smoothly pushed herself up in her leather chair and placed her arms flat on the desk top. It was a peculiar gesture and it made Gabe pause for a moment.

"Uh, anyway, he said it didn't really pan out for them," Gabe continued warily, "and this little company really tried, y'know, with a ton of promotion and everything, but I guess they're presently biting the big one and—"

"I—presently —don't —really—give—a—dirty —*damn*—what—Mr. Conet—said." Her voice had changed back to pieces of crystal, slicing through the air, stinging Gabe's face. "He has taken his leave. I am here. Me. Mis-sus Va-li-er-i. Your boss now."

Gabe pursed his lips.

Suddenly she was calm again, speaking like a mother.

"Mr. Conet was a plodder. He was slow and unproductive in his position and was not showing enough promise. I was brought in. Now, come on, Gabriel. I want us to work together here. We have to stick together. I'm sure, uh . . . Malcolm had his own modus operandi, and I have mine. And mine is for me to have much more input as to what goes on and what comes off, what comes in and what goes out. And I'm not frittering away any time in getting this back-street company on its feet again."

"I didn't know it was off 'em," Gabe said softly.

"Yes. Now, we've got to work together on this. You, me, and everyone out there." She motioned toward the closed door, down the hallway where the workrooms were situated. "Solve problems and make changes, always improving always growing. Beginning in part with your Dragons Three."

For some obscure reason, Gabe didn't know what to say to that. He just stared at the thin saffron carpet between his sneakers. There was an indistinct pulsing deep down, a feeling that what she was asking him to do was wrong. All wrong.

"Gabriel, I'm swiftly losing faith in you."

He sat up.

"Mrs. Valieri, it's not that I'm knocking your, uh, project, here, but I really can't see . . . how you're gonna make a huge killing by making all these cute and cuddly things into killers. I mean—"

"I suppose that is my problem, isn't it?" Her words were snipped at both ends. The plastoid smile had melted. It was crystal clear to Gabe that the woman did not appreciate opposing points of view. Especially from some snotty teenage freelancer who's decided to play crystalgazer for the toy's economic tidings.

Mrs. Valieri began to click her Crazy Nails on the aluminum desk. *T-tack-tick-tack-tick-tack.* "Right now, Gabe. I would like your answer. Are you in or out?" A paper-crisp finality in her voice.

tick-tack-tick-tack-tick

Gabe inhaled slowly through his nose and—

tack-tick-tack

(Give her an answer give her an answer. Are you in or out in or out or in or out hurry.)

tick-tack-tick

He looked at York.

tack-tick-tack

63

"Gabe."

tick-tack-tick

(Yes you're in. No you're out. In or out? answer please in or out? Wotsitgonna be? in or out? yes or no? toys yes money or no?)

tack-tick-tock

"Gabe."

tick-tock

"I'm . . ."

tick-tock

Looking at York.

tick-tock

Happy York. Wouldn't hurt a—

tick-tock

(mouse ran up the—)

tick

"Gabe."

tock

"I'm . . ."

tik

(just a toy yes or no yes or no or yes or no or in or out or out or in or inout inout inout inout inout inout inout inout outoutoutout)

TOK.

". . . in." Gabe said, toneless.

Mrs. Valieri slapped her hands together cheerily. The plastoid smile took form once more.

"I'm glad, Gabe. I really am, and I knew you wouldn't think of standing in the way of it."

Gabe frowned.

"A *surge,* Gabe. Ours. After all, that is what Tally-Ho means, isn't it? A surge, upward and onward. We are striving to distinguish ourselves from all the rest. I understand how you feel, but business *is* business." She tossed off the depleted truism as if it were the universal answer to any and all things and popped up from her chair. She came around the desk and took York's massive head in her hands. His sunny, alert face came right up to her calculating one.

"All right, let's have a look." She motioned to the roll of white paper at Gabe's feet. He scooped it up, twisted off the wide yellow elastic band, and unfurled the original Dragons Three design on her empty desk top. There were seven creased, dog-eared sheets meticulously specifying what goes into the construction of a bona fide Holden Dragon. Spotted and stained with assorted condiments, the first five pages were a forest of early dragon concepts: preliminary sketches, head studies, incomplete revisions—everything on the stuffed toy from the assembly of the sturdy fiberglass frame to what brand of surgical thread Gabe used, on down through the developmental stages until the last two un-soiled sheets. The full-scale diagrams of the Holden Dragon, rigid front and flank views. The finished product.

Mrs. Valieri took her pen and began to scrawl, almost carelessly, over the original design, altering the dragon to something . . . something else.

"Okay. Let's start with the expression. We can't really do anything with the eyes . . ."

(We?)

". . . but those nostrils! Let's get those flared and puffing. And get some fangs and claws. And give them *muscle!* Let's put fire into these beasts! I want them to say that they're going to eat you when you aren't looking. I want them to say they're going to eat you when you *are* looking!"

Gabe winced. She started to pull at York.

"Rip off this ridiculous fake fur and get down to Supply and pick up some green snake-pebbled latex. You know where Supply is?"

"Uh, I've made toys for Tally-Ho for over two years now."

"Okay, right, right. Now, we're going to turn these reptiles into real monsters! Give 'em anger! Give 'em fire! Give 'em . . . *chutzpah!*"

"Chutzpah?"

"Yes! And plenty of it."

And Gabe gave them plenty. She made him take them back four times before she was content. She said they were perfect. Gabe agreed. They *were* perfect. Perfectly horrific. And that pulsating feeling that the change was wrong stayed with him. (But it's only a toy. *A toy.*) And there were some major up-front bucks involved, something he was indeed in dire need of. Anyway, he completed the new Dragons Three a week ahead of schedule and could relax, coast awhile. . . .

Gabe gently dabbed the flannel rag around Sid's glass eyeballs, his nostrils, and his cruel mouth. The whole lousy, rotten Valieri business had whistled through his mind in three-quarters of a minute, tops. He could feel the anger from that day begin to percolate inside him and stopped it. He stopped it because there was no need for it and there wasn't anything he could do about it now and what-did-he-care-anyhow and—

(Surge ahead, babe, surge ahead.)

He looked at Sid.

(If this is *surging* ahead, we're in some big trouble, kids.) He dropped the rag and picked up one of the sponges and worked it around Sid's rolling shoulders and biceps. He picked up the rag again and ran it between Sid's thick fingers. He had begun to swab the dragon's chest when he stopped, puzzled. He felt a breeze on his face. Warm. It increased, decreased. It nearly felt like . . . breath. Gabe gradually raised his eyes to Sid's. Having made contact, he thought he could actually see . . . something . . . there. It was almost as if, as if Sid—

The bedroom door opened. The breeze ceased. Mom poked her face in.

"Gabe? Before I forget, can you be sure to clean out Tyler's wading pool tomorrow? It's filled with dead leaves. Okay?"

Gabe looked up at her, mouth agape. He hadn't heard what she'd said.

"Gabe?"

"Yeah?"

"Can you be sure to do that tomorrow?"

"Yeah."

"Okay. And please, really try to get along with Rachel for the next few days? Dad doesn't need the extra tension right now, okay?"

"Yeah."

"Okay. Good night, hon." She gently shut the door.

Gabe lowered his head slowly and looked into Sid's eyes for over a minute. Nothing. He placed his palm in front of the dragon's wide mouth, crammed with those jagged teeth. Nothing.

It's not time yet.

Gabe stood up and guffawed lightly. He ran his fingers through his wet hair and shook his head.

"Geez," he breathed. There was a great relief inside him, but he couldn't think of a reason why. He didn't quite know what he had been thinking.

He finished up, tossed the bag of cleaning stuff on the top shelf, and fitted the ironing board back into the closet. He slipped Sid back into his bulky body bag, laid him down with his two brothers in the rear of the closet, and closed the metal doors.

He seized an unopened bag of pickle chips hidden—from Tyler—behind his small Sony TV and grabbed an unfinished paperback off his middle bookcase shelf. He plopped down on his bed and propped up two pillows behind him. Turning to his "big box," he switched from RADIO to TAPE. Billy Squier singing "How Lonely Is the Night." He lowered the volume one level, flipped to the marked chapter in his book, and commenced munching.

Twenty-five minutes and a bag of pickle chips later, Gabe's head slipped down to his pillows. He gave a sigh, which sounded like a grunt. The horror novel, closed with Gabe's little finger between pages 176 and 177, had failed miserably in its attempt to fulfill its cover promises. In startling Vladimir Bold print, it gave its word to pound your heart, chill your spine, whiten your knuckles, and in general, mess your pants. And the critics couldn't rave enough about the grizzled author's grisly triumph.

"His best yet by far." "Utterly intoxicating." "Stiletto-tipped." "It convinced *me* 'there are such things'!" "Nothing less than the state of the art in horror fiction."

He dropped the book down the side of his bed and turned off his little Ford Model A desk lamp. Any threat of concussion forgotten, he

68

slid under the covers and pulled his huge baby-blue quilted comforter over him. He lay on his back in the dark in pre-sleep listening to Billy Squier's mournful voice. He thought about Kate.

In the area of six minutes later, he heard the click of the PLAY button coming back up, signaling the tape was finished. He rolled over to face the wall.

Right on the brink of unconsciousness, Gabe's ears picked up a sound in his room. He lay still a moment, then rolled back around and lifted his head off his pillow. His eyes strained in the stygian darkness of his room. And that's all there was: darkness. He waited for the noise to repeat itself, but all he received were the erratic yappings of the McCaffreys' miniature collie two houses down and the velvety sound of bitter night wind outside his window.

Soon, any coherent thoughts about what the noise was had been swallowed by slumber.

If Gabe had been asked about the noise, he would have said it had sounded very much as if it came from inside his closet. And that it had sounded a lot like laughing. And that it had sounded as if it were almost in . . . anticipation. He also would have said that it had sounded a lot like his imagination.

That's what he would have said if he had been asked. But he hadn't been asked. So, it did not matter a whole lot then. Not then. But it would. It would.

Four

The sun was on the brink of its escape. It had been imprisoned long enough behind the house at the end of the street.

Gabe was sprawled on the hood of his sister's flat-blue Toyota. It was a cloudless Monday morning. The beginning of another week of school. The mere thought depressed him.

He had on an old pair of beige corduroys, a brown tennis shirt, a heavy Kangaroo jacket, and his scuffed Nikes. He basically cared zero about his daily attire, unlike many of his schoolmates. He knew inside that when he really set out to dress, for a dance or whatever, he could hold his own with the best of them. Or so he'd been told. By Mom.

An immense hardcover book on Japanese animation lay beside him. Instead of pursuing females or getting hammered at somebody's party, Gabe felt there were many other things to fill his hours with. Reading, sketching, foreign films, exercising, music, and his creations. And drawing on his feet. Not that Gabe didn't like girls. He liked them. It was just that every female he had gone out with in the not-too-distant past seemed so great at first; then, too late, he would discover the girl had the personality of a used piece of Trident gum. Chewed and sugarless. And, naturally, she'd be in the same school. So, after the horrendous breakup, he'd have to pass her in the hall and sit in a desk dangerously close to her. He hated it.

Gabe sometimes fantasized about having a girl custom made for him. A female that actually conformed to his exact specifications. As in *Marionettes, Inc.* by Ray Bradbury. Kate came pretty close. As for parties, Gabe went, but you couldn't exactly call Gabriel Holden an uninhibited party animal. He sometimes wondered if there was something wrong with him. A little whacked off at the edges. A tad—retarded or something.

He gave a low chuckle when he heard the front door close.

"What's so funny, kid?" came a female voice behind him. He sat up as Rachel walked toward him. She had on an ocher sweater and slacks.

"Jus' thinkin'," Gabe said.

"About?"

"Ooohh, you know, horse, reds, acid, kinky sex, and worldwide fascism."

"Naturally. Mom says you need a ride to school. This is my day off from work. Feel incredibly lucky."

"How positively regal of you. Shall we alert the media?"

"Screw. What's wrong with your wheels?"

Gabe pointed to the mutilated ten-speed leaning against the house near the front door. "As you can see, my wild stallion has been mortally wounded."

"Yes, I see," Rachel said.

Gabe slapped his hand to his cheek.

"Astounding! The power of reason never fails to amaze me." He turned and tried to get the car door open.

"Uuhhh, your door is stuck."

"Hey, I've got an idea," Rachel said, taking out the keys from her pocket and unlocking the door.

Once inside, Rachel shifted into gear and backed out of the driveway. Beside her, Gabe twisted his head and watched the sun edge from behind the rooftop of his house and rinse the street with its light. A group of sparrows darted past.

Gabe turned on the car radio. Nazareth. He cranked it. Rachel clicked it off.

"Heyy," Gabe said.

"My car, deary," Rachel said.

He hated it when she did that. Mostly because she was right.

Not taking her eyes off the road, Rachel motioned to the book in Gabe's lap.

"What're you reading?"

"Ego Gratification through Violence," Gabe said, and put the book on the other side of him so she couldn't see the real title. "I think you read it."

Rachel shook her head and said something Gabe couldn't hear.

"So. Why *did* you attack me last night?" Gabe asked, a couple of minutes later.

"I didn't!"

"No, I'd really like to know."

"Get off it, Gabe," she warned.

"Was it a sudden impulse?"

"You want to get dumped off right here?" she said, dead serious.

Gabe faced the front.

"Was it my English Leather?" he asked.

Rachel shook her head hopelessly.

"Crud," she said.

"You often talk about yourself in the third person?" Gabe asked.

He smiled. She didn't.

Reaching his corner, Rachel smoothly pulled her Toyota over. Gabe hopped out.

"Thank you very little, darling."

"Gabe, the pleasure was unequivocally all yours."

"Love you, too, pooch."

"Adulation will get you absolutely nowhere."

"Huh. There's nowhere I absolutely want to get with you, believe me. Toodles!"

Gabe slammed the car door, cutting off what she said next. Getting a better grip on his heavy book, he blew her a kiss and headed for ol' J. L. Lloyd.

"Ernest Defarge was, as a youth in Paris, a servant of Dr. Manette. And so, having been treated with consideration, he retains a modicum of . . ."

Mr. Bergent paced slowly up and down the aisles in the brightly lit English room. He held a hardcover edition of *A Tale of Two Cities* in front of him. He was a ruddy-complexioned man in his mid-twenties with a narrow build. He had a long, sinister black moustache that always reminded Gabe of the nefarious villain in the old *Perils of Pauline* adventures. He had been, in a way, gunning for Gabe ever since he had caught the boy with two pages full of drawings of him in a long black coat and top hat, tormenting

73

some luscious blond with a number of inventive techniques. Gabe could have gotten away with it if he hadn't put "Mr. B" beside each and every one. The man was very touchy in that area.

He was five aisles away from Gabe's row. By choice, Gabe sat at the last desk in the farthest corner of the room, overlooking an empty street.

Gabe was not listening to what the English teacher was saying. He had seen the 1917 and the 1935 film versions on TV and knew how the thing ended. His mind was centered on the images he had almost completed in his coil notebook. The Dragons Three.

Mr. Bergent was four aisles away now.

Gabe drew York, Sid, and Hubub together, arms around each other.

Three aisles away.

Gabe's pencil moved in small, spasmodic movements. He started to whistle through his teeth.

Two aisles.

Gabe stared down at his small accomplishment. He began to add shading.

One aisle.

Picture completed, Gabe bounced his eraser up and down on his desk top. Resting his head in his right hand, he gazed out the window. He saw the sun was enjoying its freedom. He spotted a group of sparrows that had congregated on a telephone wire. A doubling back of scenes. For no reason whatsoever, Gabe's mind jumped back to the Pumpkin-X concert, the white explosion, and . . . the sparrows. The sparrows that had been there. But they weren't *there* anymore. They were . . .

(Here . . . ?)

Gabe sniggered stiffly and winced.

(Cut it out! That is duuummmb!)

But it wasn't so dumb. And Gabe knew it because he could feel something, almost grasp it. It was muffled, deep inside him. A slurred whispering in his mind. Messages. Questions. An agitating perception of something, bordering on déjà vu. He knew it, but then again, he didn't.

Frowning, he stared again at the little birds. The group was unmoving and seemed, to Gabe, to be looking in the school building's direction. No. They were all looking in the window's direction. In Gabe's direction. At . . . Gabe.

"Gabriel."

Mr. Bergent's voice was akin to a searing electrical charge. Gabe jumped slightly, hoping no one noticed. His mind raced through mud. He looked up stupidly into the English teacher's face.

"Yeah?"

Giggles from somewhere in the room.

"Houston to Major Holden." A low voice, cupped in hands, from somewhere else.

Mr. Bergent looked down at the trio of dragons who stared up at them both. The English teacher worked the muscles of his jaw.

Mr. Bergent slowly ripped the drawing from the coils of Gabe's notebook. To Gabe, the painful poppings were like little explosions resounding through the room. The English teacher held the drawing up.

"Ah, Mr. Artist, what's our contribution today? Oh, how cute. You are so talented. Now how about answering the question for us." He said it all in one breath.

"The . . . question?"

More giggles. Red was working itself into Gabe's cheeks.

Mr. Bergent gave Gabe a dead look.

"Ernest Defarge was the leader of what underground movement?"

Gabe brought the question to the front of his mind, which was a useless act since he didn't have the foggiest idea what the answer was.

"Gabriel."

"Yes?"

"The answer?"

"Uh, I dunno."

"You dunno."

"No."

"I was sure yesterday I assigned the chapter that has something to do with the answer to the question."

"I guess I didn't read it."

"You guess?"

"I didn't read it."

"So there is no guessing about it."

"I guess not."

The giggling was unending.

"Getting back to the question at hand. Would I be correct in saying that you do not know the answer to it?"

"Uh, you would and I don't."

"You don't have the barest inkling as to what the answer is?"

"That's about it."

The giggling stopped. The silence in the room was stifling. Gabe sat rock still and stared at his pencil.

(Go away, Bergent. Oh, please go away. I've

had enough, really. I'll be good. Go away and torment some other poor soul.)

Bergent didn't go away. He just stood there, forearms on Gabe's desk, staring at him for a million and one years. Then he turned to the rest of the room.

"Well, what do you think, people? A little stupid?"

A couple of kids said, "Yeah."

"Apply a little logic next time, Gabriel," the English teacher said, and in one movement he crumpled the dragons in his large pink hand, scooped up his textbook, turned on his heel, and strode up the aisle.

Exhaling a stream of air, Gabe looked back outside at the sparrows.

The telephone line was empty.

Naturally.

When the final buzzer of the day sounded, Gabe went out to the student parking lot. He didn't feel up to the trek all the way home today. Jimmy and his ivory chariot were absent, so he had to search out someone with a running auto who was going his way. Eunice was going his way. Even before he asked her for the lift, even before he made eye contact, he knew she was going to conclude he was trying to start something deadly serious with her. It had nothing to do with the almighty ego. Far from it. It was just the way the shy ones felt about him. But Gabe didn't care. All he wanted was a ride home. A male can get a ride with a member of the opposite gender without making plans as to what vegetable they're going to serve at their wedding reception, Gabe thought.

It wasn't so bad. She had an 8-track tape deck in the car and inserted the soundtrack to Barbra Streisand's *Yentl*. She was a huge fan. It wasn't so bad. Then she began to sing along with it. It wasn't so bad. Then she made Gabe join in. It got bad.

The Holden house was a two-story with beige hardboard siding. Walking up the lawn to the front door, Gabe caught sight of a small group of dark sparrows situated on the television antenna. There was no movement to them. He squinted.

They were like stones balanced on the antenna. Gabe gaped up at them, searching. The slurred whispering in his mind was back: active unsubstantial queries. Not to be answered here, not to be answered now. But there was an *awareness* in him. An awareness of messages, something, something he should know, should realize. He could almost, almost understand. . . .

He didn't have clue one. He just did . . . not . . . know.

Then, as if in an effort to push the incomprehensible whispering back and out of his mind, he raised his hand and waved up at them.

"Yo."

It was a moronic gesture, pointless. The birds stared down at him. He wondered how long they were going to keep his stare. Or how long he was going to keep *theirs*. They didn't let go. Finally, Gabe yielded. He pursed his lips and left them.

Shutting the front door behind him, he kicked in his shoes with the rest of the family's on the tile floor of the foyer. The whole house was swathed in the heavy, undeniable aroma of steak from the oven. The mouth-watering smell was almost tangible. He could hear Mom's and Rachel's voices bickering in the kitchen. He took a few steps over to the entrance.

Mom was sitting at the table, hands interlaced, and Rachel was standing, drying cutlery with a checkered dish towel. The dishwasher was on the fritz, so the dishes had to be done the old way. Manually. Rachel was tossing the knives and forks into the kitchen drawer so hard it sounded like two knights in heavy armor doing battle with broadswords and maces.

Clank.

"—telling you, I am through with Eric," Rachel said. "Just get used to it. It's my decision."

Clank.

"Rachel, how in the world can you be so cold? So callous? Eric loves you," Mom urged. "This is hurting him so. He told me. He almost started to cry."

Clank.

"Oh, hey, wonderful." Rachel threw up her hands. "A crybaby wimp for a boyfriend. A real strong supporter. Look, you and Eric get along just hunky-dory. Real pals from day one. Aaannd you've decided that we should get married. How sweet. It's what you want. What *you* want. Well, dear mother, what about what Rachel wants?"

Clank.

"I really don't think Rachel knows . . . what she wants," Mom said.

CLANK.

"No! No! Rachel knows what she wants and what she doesn't want! And what she *doesn't*

79

want is that dumpy, carrot-topped, drooling excuse for a—"

Her words sat in the air as Gabe glided into the kitchen. Very deliberately, he opened the refrigerator, decided on a McIntosh apple and a hunk of marble cheese, and backed out.

"We now return you to your regular programming," Gabe said from the hall. "Thank you."

He trudged upstairs, making skuff-skuff sounds with his feet. He had learned a long time ago that his sister was a very predictable person. Almost monotonous. In school she had consistently come through with flying colors in math, chemistry, social studies, and other such hellish classes. But when it came to art or any other subject that involved the "theater of the mind," something Gabriel excelled in, she was nothing, El Zilcho. And once out of school, it was the same old scene. Highly prosaic schedule: sleep, eat, work; sleep, eat, work. She had passed up college for a career in cosmetics at a large downtown shopping mall. So she could sit at home and wait for Handsome Hubby to come and sweep her away to the suburban castle where all her aspirations would finally come true. Yes, the regulation picket fence, the two kiddies, the big dog, the station wagon with the wooden sides, the geraniums, the higher tax bracket, "General Hospital," "All My Children," and Luke and Laura and Jenny and Greg and—

Tyler, on the other hand, was the complete opposite. The kid had a whole motion-picture company up in his skull. He was H. G. Wells, Stan Lee, and George Lucas all wrapped up in one four-foot package. Epic intergalactic tales of good against evil amid glittering megacities in the galaxy's molecular nuclei went on in his room every day. He was brimming with surprises constantly. A fact Gabe would be reminded of in about three minutes.

He had just about entered his bedroom when he heard the distant click. He turned. No author of the sound was there. He kicked the door shut behind him and threw his jacket down on the floor with the stuff that was already there. He turned on the radio. Jethro Tull.

Gabe's bedroom was very similar to any other teenage boy's bedroom. It was small, it was his, and the door locked. As was to be expected, there were pictures everywhere: One-sheets, the poster-sized advertisements posted in theater windows. Near the ceiling, fantasy masterpieces by Frazetta, Corben, and the Brothers Hildebrandt. Then there was his "No Lifeguard on Duty" sign, his "It's Always Darker Before It's Pitch Black" and "Nuke the Whale" posters. Taking up the wall next to his bed was a photo mural, taken from the moon's surface, of an "earthrise" in endless space.

His finished three-shelf bookcase was filled with soft- and hardcover works by Edgar Rice Burroughs, Robert E. Howard, Arthur C. Clarke, Stephen King, and of course, Ray Bradbury. On the top of the case, open, was a copy of Philip K. Dick's *Do Androids Dream of Electric Sheep?*

A sizable sheet of two-ply Bristol paper was taped at the corners to the smooth white surface of his drafting table. A great woolly beast

81

that could be described as part slug and part manatee stared back from the paper. It had eight flat, gangly arms, two eyes that bulged out like pieces of fruit, and a snout that ended with what looked like a clown's nose. Gabe called it Maurice the Hossenfeffer. He was thinking of hollowing out its back and converting it into a portable baby crib. It could go places.

Gabe took a mouthful of apple and dipped his hand into the drafting table's pencil tray. It was brimming with uncapped felt pens, pencils chewed to the leads, erasers rubbed almost to extinction, and multicolored pencil shavings. Munching loudly, he grabbed a soft-lead pencil and rotated it quickly in a little silver sharpener. Gabe bit off another hunk and brought up the pencil. The fine tip of the lead hadn't quite touched paper when the door to his room crashed open. Chunks of apple burst from Gabe's mouth, spattering Maurice.

"APOCALYPSE NOW! YAAAAAAAAAAA-AAAAA!!"

Screaming, arms waving wildly above his head, Gabe dove off his stool and rolled under the table. Then he heard the giggling. Tyler. The tawney-haired, almost frail boy stood in the doorway, sneakered feet wide apart. He had on a Green Beret outfit, complete with ascot, the cap tilted to one side. He had one of Dad's old buck knives on his hip. He was holding his hands behind him and looked very tough.

It was Gabe's turn to giggle. He was still giggling right up until Tyler brought out what he was holding behind his back. Gabe bolted up.

"Cap'n Crunch almighty! That's Dad's gun, you little dolt!"

"Ssshhh, c'mon, Mom'll *hear you*," Tyler said.

"Mom'll *kill you* if she sees you waving that around."

"It isn't loaded."

"Well, she's still gonna blow a gasket. How did you know where it was?"

"Come on, how long can anybody keep anything from anybody for any amount of time a secret from anybody in this house?"

"Fairly confusingly put, Ty, but what *were* you doing in the top drawer of Mom and Dad's dresser?"

"I'm gonna need Dad's piece for my Futura party next week and—"

"You little turdcake!" Gabe shrieked, looking at the pieces of apple on his drawing. "You're dead!"

Gabe started to move on Tyler. The kid had the buck knife out in a flash, holding the blade high.

"Back off, suckah, or—"

Gabe grabbed the knife away from him.

"No! No more knives! I can't take it!" Gabe barked. "What is this getup?"

"Gimme," Tyler said, taking the knife from Gabe and slipping it back in its sheath. He put the gun in his belt. He put his hands on his hips.

"You like?" he asked.

"Yeah, yeah, it looks great, but where'd you get it?"

Tyler strode arrogantly into the room. He leaned up against the far wall, pulled out the polished .38 and flipped out the cylinder as if to make sure it was loaded. He looked very professional. Gabe rolled his eyes.

"Traded. Well, I don't get to keep it, but I got it for a week. I traded with this guy in school. He wanted the first ten issues of *New Mutants*. I got doubles of that, so it doesn't matter. Pretty good, huh?"

"Shrewd beyond belief," Gabe said, picking pieces of fruit off his drawing.

"Uh, sorry 'bout that."

"Yeah, yeah."

"Uh, Mrs. Hamond is givin' this party in her class next week. It's kind of a part Halloween, part what-you're-going-to-be-when-you-grow-up thing."

"I thought you said you wanted to be a movie director. Like Spielberg and Coppola and all the greats."

"Well, for this party, I'd rather be impressive than honest. And a mercenary is impressive, right?"

"Whatever," Gabe said, taking the ruined picture off the table.

"You're not comin' to Richard's wedding this weekend?"

"Nope, gotta work."

"I'm sure you feel real bad about that, huh?"

"Shattered."

Gabe pulled out another sheet of paper from underneath the table and taped it onto the drawing board.

"You gonna hafta do it again?" Tyler asked.

"I'm gonna hafta do it again."

"Sorry."

"You said that."

"Well, I am."

"I didn't like it the way it was, anyway."

"Oh. What is it, anyway."

"Maurice the Hossenfeffer."

Tyler stumbled out of the room, holding onto his stomach with laughter. Gabe kicked his door shut. *He* couldn't believe he had said that with a straight face. He picked up the pencil again, sharpened it, and commenced sketching.

Somewhere around an hour later, Gabe sat back from his vulture position over his drafting table.

"Fini," he breathed, dropping the fountain pen back into the tray. The drawing was done boldly in a black India ink. He had changed the overall look of Maurice from the grotesque, misshapen thing it had been to more of a big, innocent, roly-poly critter a kid could be buddies with. But Gabe knew Valieri was going to shoot it down if he didn't make some drastic changes. Hostile, Gabe, hostile. Surge ahead.

He picked up the smudged art gum and began to erase the lines of lead that had strayed from the drawing itself. He touched the gum to the paper, gently rubbing out the—

"Get out, Daddy." Behind him.

Gabe spun on his stool.

(Get out, Daddy? Where've I heard that befo— The shower. Yeah, but—)

"Get out, Daddy." It was a vicious hiss and it came from within his closet.

Gabe stood up with a bored look on his face.

"Yeah, yeah, very boring stuff, Tyler. Yeah, you got in there and I didn't hear you. We're all proud," Gabe said to the closed closet. "Getcher little butt outa there, twerp."

No movement. A commercial for electronic security was on the radio.

"I mean it, kiddo, or there's gonna be some major-league trouble comin' your way in about one second," Gabe said, reaching out to grasp the metal flower knobs of his closet. His index finger and thumb had just touched the knobs when his bedroom door opened and Tyler's face peered around.

"Supper," the little boy said. "What're you doin'?"

Gabe took his hands away and a tiny icicle skipped down his spine.

"Nothing," Gabe said, too fast. "Umm, Tyler . . ."

"What?"

"Uhh, nothing."

"You said that."

Gabe shoved the little boy's face out of the doorway. He snatched a last look at the closet and stepped into the hallway, closing his door behind him. He stood there for a moment, feet at awkward angles. He let his fingers slip from the doorknob and followed Tyler down the stairs. Wondering.

After a quiet supper of boneless steak, diced potatoes, and hot apple pie with vanilla ice cream melting on top, Gabe dried the dishes, watched an hour of prime-time television with the family in the living room, did fifty-three sit-ups, watched some more of the tube in his room, and crashed. But not before he took a look-see in his closet. Just a quick one. He found nothing out of order. Never expected to, he told himself. Never expected.

Gabe stared at the ceiling in the dark. It was a mile distant. He squeezed his eyes shut, then snapped them open again.

Something had woken him up, but he didn't have the foggiest what. He waited patiently. Nothing. He allowed his eyes to droop shut, half expecting the sound to come again just before he fell asleep.

And it did. A crackling.

(What was that?)

He went tense. His ears sharpened to pick up anything else. Nothing. There was nothing but the soft roaring sound of dead air. Aggravating pinpricks spread over his moist skin. He closed his eyes again.

Right on cue the crackling came again. Stopped.

A thin tide of fear washed up over him. The whites of his eyes stood out in the dark room. He was wrapped up in his quilted comforter so that only his face showed. His eyes locked on to the dim outline of his closet door.

A featherlight click cleaved the quiet like a hot knife through fresh pumpkin pie. His body froze in bed.

(I heard that! I heard that! I heard what? What th'hell did I hear?!!)

Visions of horrible death bounced into his head. Michael from *Halloween.* He came through a window downstairs. Jason from *Friday the 13th.* He got through a back door. Norman from *Psycho.* He got tired of waiting down in the fruit cellar. Shimmering kitchen knives looking for white flesh.

(Waitaminnit. We don't have a fruit cellar.)

A sound. Brushing. Something brushing against the shag carpet of his room.

Before Gabe's horrified saucer eyes, his closet doors were inching slooooooooowly open.

(I'm not seeing this. No sir, I AM NOT SEEING THIS.)

His eyes were riveted to what he wasn't seeing. His mind was Cream of Wheat. He could not move. Paralyzed. There was nothing between brain and toes. He stared unwillingly into the darkness of his closet. He couldn't see any distinct movement. Nothing came out.

He blinked.

(. ... What . . . opened it? . . . How . . . did it open all by itsel—)

Something came out.

A shape. Big, black, and hunched over. It seemed to be standing at the opening of the closet, braced between the folded doors. Gabe could hardly make it out. Then it moved out and he lost track of it altogether.

(Whereisit?!!whereisitwhereisitwhereisitwhereisit!! wherediditgo?!!!)

His mind was an unending chitter-chatter.

He clutched at his sheets, pulling, pulling.

His insides were alive, shrieking.

(Nonononononononononononononononopleasepleasenotmenotmenotme.)

He wanted to jump up and tear out of the room.

(I can't!)

He wanted to scream.

(I—I can't!!)

He wanted to cry.

(That'd be helpful.)

He wanted Mom.

(Wottaman!)

Abruptly, he found the shape again. Right bang in front of him. It just stood there, hunched over. Gabe thought he could almost see its eyes. Large round glittering billiard balls.

Gabe made a frantic effort to rise, but he felt a heavy force pushing down on him.

(Hands?)

It was pushing him down onto his back. But when it had done so it kept up the tremendous weight, as if to push Gabe right through the very mattress of his bed. His breath was being painfully squeezed out of him.

He was being slowly deflated. His nerves were screaming bloody murder. With an incredible effort, he managed to move his lips and speak.

". . . help . . ."

He was helpless, utterly helpless. Then he heard the voice.

"Get out, Father. Go with them and stay out." The words were so low-pitched and leaden that Gabe thought he could actually feel the rumbling vibrations in his chest cavity. He was crushed farther and farther down until—

It's not time yet.

Gabe jerked up in the blackness. It felt as if he had left his head behind. He couldn't catch his breath, started to gag. He was lost, so lost. He was falling and falling. He groped for a handhold. He couldn't recognize anything. His mind whirled, trying to land.

(I am in . . . where? . . . my bed in . . . where? . . . my room in . . . where? . . . my house.)

He felt his hairless chest with his hand.

(A nightmare. It was a nightmare. Was it? Was I asleep? Yes. No. Yes, had to be. Yeah, yeah, was asleep. Gone. La-la land. I had a nightmare, a real beaut. Y'okay, okay, just hold on.)

Naked except for his blue briefs, Gabe got to his feet like a ninety-year-old man. He stood up from the floor. He couldn't recall rolling off his bed and hitting the floor, but that didn't matter much at the moment. A reverberating timpani festival was in full swing inside his head. The carpet felt like cool straw under his bare feet. Feeling along the walls, he made his way down the hallway to the bathroom. Plugged into the hall outlet, Tyler's Incredible Hulk night light glowed green on his ankles as he shuffled by, toes snapping and popping.

Coming upon the open doorway of the bathroom, he flicked on the light. It seared viciously into his brain. After checking behind the door and in the shower, and feeling like a pinhead for doing it, Gabe bent over the sink. He splashed cold water over his face. It dripped down from his bangs. He cupped his shaking hands and gulped the water greedily before it leaked through his thin fingers. It went down nastily.

Padding back to his room, Gabe halted and turned. He looked back to the end of the hallway, at the closed door of his parents' bedroom. He rubbed the back of his slick neck.

(What are you thinking? What are you thinking? Aren't you a tad too old for the "It was only a bad dream and it's all in your noggin" bit? Get back to your room, you stupid dork! Travel, now!)

Holding a hand over his eyes, Gabe turned on

the big light in his room. It was cold. He darted a look at his closet. He knew sooner or later he was going to have to do it if he was going to get any kind of sleep before daylight surfaced.

He didn't have an inkling as to what the dream meant. All he knew was it was the third time he had been referred to as a Daddy and told to get out. The first time, by Rachel in the shower. Second time, when he was at his drafting table and it had come from his closet. That *must* have been Tyler. It just sounded as if it had come from his closet. And the third time, in his nightmare. Coincidence, that's all it was, a bizarre happenstance. It didn't relate to anything.

He stepped in front of his closed closet. The beating of his heart increased to a pummeling behind his rib cage. Nostrils dilating, he gripped the metal flower knobs. It became something he had to do. Half preparing for a speedy retreat, he pulled the closet wide open.

The slight draft that he created caused two coat hangers to gently collide. That was all. His shoulders stood at ease.

(Nope, nothing wrong here, General.)

Gabe's mind jumped back to the countless mid-century oriental radiation-monster flicks he had sneaked on the "Late Late Movie" in his younger years.

(Right. Nothing wrong here. Then the giant mutant what-have-you leaps out in glorious 3-D and proves once again you can't get good help nowadays.)

Gabe parted his clothes and inspected the bottom of his closet. The ironing board, barbells, half-filled boxes of never-returned school library books, coverless magazines, tattered DC comics, torn posters, and assorted lacerated records. A pile of pop cans in one corner of the closet spread over to crumpled balls of paper, scattered cassette tapes, a drained 7-Up bottle on its side, perforated socks, pencils, pens, and so on and so forth.

Crammed into the dingy right corner of the closet were two florid pasteboard boxes, the original residences of a potato chip shipment and children's winter boots. The boxes were now heavily ladened with mustard-yellow fiberglass tubing and generous sheets of deep green foam and hides of pebbled latex. Sitting on top were flip-open bonbon boxes chock-full with oval vermilion eyes of glass and intact sets of ivory plastic teeth fashioned after those of a tiger shark. And in the face of all this, the Dragons Three. From out of their translucent body bags, the three of them looked up at him as if to ask if they could come out now.

Gabe stood on his toes and took a quick peek at his top shelf. The plastic bag of cleaning stuff, four ski sweaters too small for him, a depleted pillow, a thin yellowing quilt, a relish jar full of pennies and nickels, an empty Cherry Glosettes box, a bongo drum, more posters, and dunes of dust.

(Jerko. A case of the almighty heebie-jeebies, fer sure.)

Leaving the closet open, Gabe whacked off the light. Blackness. He half tripped, half shoulder-rolled into bed, yanked the covers over him, and was soon asleep. There were no more dreams for him that night. Or for the rest of the week.

There was a lacuna, a breathing spell, a calmness, an interim exempt from crushing nightmares, voices from the closet, shower ambushes, and any and all other "bizarre happenstances." Standard peace reigned in the Holden household.

Gabe had heard the rumbling voice telling him to get out, but he did not listen to it. It was going to cause him a lot of misery someday.

Five

Mom was fluttering up the stairs, back down again, into the kitchen, out again, then up the stairs again, muttering away to herself. Her dove-colored raincoat billowed behind her. Dad came in the front door. He had already readied the forest-green Pontiac for their trip to Richard's wedding. Tyler was in the back seat playing Zaxxon, and Rachel was behind the steering wheel, waiting.

It was twenty after seven on a very chilly, very dismal Saturday morning. They had planned to leave by six o'clock sharp, but the alarm from a clock just wasn't enough to push the blood to the essential places in the body human. They had overslept. This had tossed Mom all off, instilling in her that nagging feeling that she had forgotten something.

Gabe was perched on the arm of the love seat in his black terrycloth robe. His face was buried in his hands. He had risen to see them off and was not fully conscious yet.

"Where is she?" Dad asked wearily.

"Upstairs, downstairs, everywheres."

"Mariiie! We're leaving now or not at all," Dad called.

Mom called back that she was "coming, coming." Dad turned to Gabe.

"Gabe."

Gabe looked up. He was wearing an old pair of mirrored Foster Grants. He couldn't deal with the sun's glaring rays that early in the day. He moaned as Dad pulled them off.

"Okay, you have Donna's phone number?" Dad asked.

"C'mon, you're comin' back tonight," Gabe said, taking the sunglasses back.

"Well, you never know."

Mom flew back down the stairs, securing a pink silk scarf high on her neck.

"We should be home, hmmmm, around midnight," Dad said, looking at his watch.

Mom came up and took off Gabe's Foster Grants. He moaned.

"Okay, Gabe, before or after you go to work, can you clean out Tyler's pool? I asked you last week," she said.

"Fine."

"And make sure the house is locked."

"Right."

"And we should be home, hmmmm, around midnight."

"So I hear."

"Aaannnd . . ." She leaned over and gave Gabe a wet peck on the left cheek. "Bye, honey."

"Hey, y'all be sure to give a big howdy from yours truly to all our shirttail kin, y'hear?" Gabe said in a pretty pathetic drawl.

"They aren't *that* distant, Gabe," Dad said over his shoulder.

From the doorway, Gabe watched the Pontiac

back out of the driveway. It was cold outside and he could see his breath. Rachel stuck her tongue out at him. He gestured at her in Italian. He waved feebly at the rest of them as the car accelerated down the empty street.

He trudged back upstairs. He pulled his pleated curtains closed and looked at the LED display on his clock radio: 7:35. He set the alarm to go off at 8:05. That would give him plenty of time before work. Not bothering to take off his robe or his Foster Grants, he pulled the covers over himself and went to sleep.

His head bounced off his pillow when the alarm went off at the designated time. Sunglasses hanging off one ear, he brought his hand down and missed. Tried again and bull's-eye. He pretty near smashed the little machine, not to mention his hand. He then began his morning aerobics: violently falling out of bed and stumbling into the bathroom.

After a speedy, scalding shower, he put his robe back on and went downstairs. The house was frigid, but he didn't touch the thermostat because the sun was coming up fast and it was the Spartan thing to do. He poured himself a tall frosty glass of concentrated orange juice, and a heaping bowl of Pebbles cereal, grabbed a frosted Pop-Tart, and went into the living room. Broad strips of warm yellow light came through the floral patterns of the drapes across the bay window, which faced the street, and across the sliding door, which led out to the backyard.

He walked back into the family room and lugged a deep, sand-colored chair over into the living room, in front of the TV. He pushed the heavy oak coffee table just ahead of him. Via remote control, he turned the console on and crossed his feet on the table, an act punishable by death if Mom ever caught him. He chuckled through a half hour of ancient Warner Brothers animation and ran back upstairs to get dressed.

In front of the spacious mirror in his parents' bedroom he blow-dried his hair into some kind of shape, then skipped back to his room, ripping off his robe. He ransacked his middle dresser drawer for a clean shirt. He pulled out a tight black T-shirt with CONAN THE BARBARIAN in loud white letters across the chest. He turned and whipped open his closet for a pair of jeans, and something heavy rolled onto his feet. Startled, he danced a fancy step back.

Hubub. His eyes were on, glowing red, standing out in the dimness of the room. He grinned up at Gabe from behind the transparent body bag. Gabe did not grin back. He frowned. Obviously someone had turned his eyes on. And Gabe didn't have to guess who. As he bent down to turn them off, he twisted his head to the open closet. Deep in the back, four more diamonds of scarlet flame were ignited. York's and Sid's eyes were also on. They shone the way a cat's eyes do when they catch the headlights of a car coming down a street at night. But there was no street and no car here; this was just Gabe's closet.

"Thanks a bunch, Rachel, you scuzzbag," Gabe muttered.

He flicked off Hubub's switch, did the same to Sid, and was reaching out to York's head when he stopped. Gabe looked at York and York *looked* back, blood-red eyes unblinking. Or so it very well seemed. Eerie. The air in the room went very cold, penetrating. Trails of goose bumps swirled over Gabe's flesh, making his hair stand to attention. For a fifth of a second, not even that, he thought he had actually seen York's green leathery eyelids move together, slowly narrowing his eyes into glittering ruby slits. They had a "don't you even think about it" look. And what was worst of all was that *York didn't have eyelids.* Gabe hadn't made him with any.

York *didn't* have any eyelids and they *hadn't* moved together. Gabe knew that. But he still found it easy to imagine that he did have some and they had done that. He found it real easy. Almost, maybe . . . *too* easy.

He stretched out his hand again to turn the eyes off. From out of nowhere his battering heart began to crawl up to his throat as he reached behind York's head. He hesitated. The eyes glowed red on his bent fingers. His scalp was alive, prickling.

It felt the same as reaching out to pet a big strange dog who's just lying there and isn't panting and isn't wagging and is absolutely inert but his attentive rich red eyes are *fixed* on you, on your face, on your *eyes,* and there's a crowd of people standing around who have run out of things to talk about and are now watching you with this big dog, and the "don't you even think about it" look in the rich red eyes is replaced by "go ahead, pet me, go ahead, pet me, go ahead, you have to, everybody's watching you, go ahead, pet me, I'm watching you, so g'head and pet me, g'head, just do it, just do it, do it, do it, do it, do it, Do it, Do it, DO IT, DO IT, *DO IT—*"

He did it and took his hand back. The two miniature light bulbs changed back to a pale maroon.

He hoisted Hubub back in with the other two. He pulled a clean pair of powder-blue jeans off a metal hanger and slid the closet shut. He exhaled a rush of hot air through his nose and ran his fingers through his not-yet-dry hair. He loosened out and felt something fall away from him. Not fear, but something indecipherable, something like, like . . .

(Whaaat?)

Well, there *was* fear, but something else was present. He couldn't give it a title. He shook his head, eyes closed. He blamed what he thought he had seen on nasty tricks played by darkness and ye old imagination.

"Together again, mesdemoiselles et messieurs et all the lil' chillins, for your personal thrills and chillsssss."

He snorted and shook his head again.

"Get a grip, Holden," he said loudly, pulling on his jeans. He scooped up his wallet off his dresser, snapped on his watch, grabbed his khaki-green jacket, and bounded down the stairs.

He stepped outside and played with the brass front doorknob to make sure it was locked. He pulled up his jacket collar as an ice-water breeze flipped up his hair. The sky was somber, heavy with massive indigo clouds tediously pushing their way across. Crossing the lawn, he looked up and, yes, there they were. His eyes narrowed coldly. Taking up the center of the strip of telephone line that hung between two poles were the sparrows. The line swayed with the wind, but they sat tight, their dot-eyes downward.

It came again. Muddled, papery whispering in the head, nagging him, telling him, *telling* him.

(No!)

He shook his head in four quick semicircles, trying to rid himself of some obscure cobwebs that wouldn't go away. For the life of him, he just couldn't make out the mumbling in his brain and so didn't know what any of it meant. And until it elucidated itself on its own, he wasn't going to let it drive him insane. The little feathered group had been materializing uncannily all week, like that one single person you do not want to meet up with but shows up all the same. They were there without fail—outside English class, science class, art class, a 7-Eleven, the public library, Lee's house when he was there on Thursday. And it wasn't as if they were following him, because he never once saw them in flight. He would look up or turn around and, wotta-ya-know, there they were with their incessant head-whispers. But it wasn't *their* whispers. They didn't have thing one to do with the whispers, Gabe had told himself simply. They weren't even whispers. Just soft headaches, thazzall. It's not as if the sparrows were, were *talking* to him, he had said out loud once, jokingly. Maybe twice. *It's not like the sparrows were talking to him.* Talking to him. Telling him . . . warning . . . him . . .

(Warning me? Warning me?! What is this?)

Gabe gritted his teeth and shook his head, like a wet puppy drying itself off. He cleared
100

away that screwy line of asinine thought. That was crazy, idiotic, absurd.

"RUH-DICULOUS!" he said theatrically. Then he shut up and looked around at the windows of the houses on the opposite side of the street. He felt it was a miracle the gents in pressed whites hadn't been called in yet. How long had he been standing there on the lawn and what had he been doing?

He gave the sparrows a stiff little two-finger salute, trotted down to the south end of the street, and headed left. Since he still hadn't picked up the new tires for his ten-speed, he would have to catch the bus to work. He jogged down another block to the timeworn bus stop bench, plopped down cross-legged, and waited for the scheduled arrival of the great rolling silver and blue hunk of steel.

When Gabe returns tonight he will wish to God Mr. Joyoki had taken his vacation during the summer.

Six

Gabe's beloved shift finally came to its end at five. Sam, habitually dilatory, showed up ten minutes later. Gabe tore down to the bicycle shop three stores over, picked up two new ten-speed tires, and vaulted onto the already moving bus. He instructed the driver to "put both feet on it." He reached the Q-Dome Mall fifteen minutes later and hustled his buns up and over to Soaring Records, where Kate was just being relieved from her shift. Perfect timing. Perfect girl.

All the way over on the bus, Gabe had silently called himself every possible obscene term known to man. He was about to sup with the girl of his lifetime—we're talking *lifetime* here; anything else has *got* to be a letdown—and he was wearing CONAN THE BARBARIAN across his chest. Brilliant. You just don't do that. But his apprehension swiftly decreased when he saw Kate. Her coal-black hair was pulled back in a tight braid, thin strands curling down each temple. She had dog tags around her throat and was wearing a baggy angora sweater, a turquoise miniskirt, and a pair of Adidas, no socks. She had the cinnamon legs of a ballerina. Later, she would tell him she was taking classes.

She had already picked out the place for them to dine. It was in the mall. Since it was Saturday night, everything stayed open until nine. She led him in and out of her personal shortcuts to the restaurant. It was at the very end of the building. A tiny place tucked away at the back of a short cul-de-sac. It served up health food meals with an Italian twist. They sat down at a round enameled driftwood table in the far corner. Hidden stereo speakers seeped Spandau Ballet. Kate ate there all the time, so she ordered for the both of them. Gabe ate everything on his plates and tasted nothing.

Their conversation was gloriously aimless. Parents, jobs, *Dune, Gremlins,* the Pumpkin-X concert, New Wave, Sting, Pia Zadora, kids at school, cocaine, cops, her Catholic church, and the drawings on Gabe's feet, which he displayed for her on the table.

Gabe told her about the time he and his family went on a two-week fishing trip to Alaska and how he was chased down the bank of the river, in bare feet, by a brown bear. Kate told him about the time she and a girlfriend went on a two-week sightseeing trip in Barbados and how they were chased down the streets of Bridgetown at night, in high heels, by a pimp.

Nearing the end of dessert, the conversation rolled around to the inevitable subject.

"Dragons?"

"Dragons."

"Bitchin'."

"You really think so?"

"I really think so."

Seeing she was genuinely interested, Gabe told her how he had first fallen for the old story

103

of "Hey! Lookee-lookee! You too can make big bucks at home!" And there was no stopping him. It all gushed out and Kate listened, quietly chewing on a slice of seed bread.

He told her about the long line of creatures weird and wonderful he had created before the Dragons Three. He told her how, since acquiring the ability to turn pages, he had kept a personal collection of the big lizards, along with vampires, werewolves, Pegasus, the Thing, Bilbo Baggins, and Thumper, in a sectioned pasture in the back of his mind. Told her how four and a half determined months ago he had chosen three of his dragons and brought them out of that pasture and solidified them.

He told her how, long, long, long ago, in the craggy Celtic highlands, a gaunt, bearded poet would graphically embroider tales of horror and mystery 'round a crackling campfire. Tightly wrapping their bare arms around their knees, pressing them up against their chests, tribesmen would listen bug-eyed to his fearsome black narratives of one-hundred-foot monsters diving out of the thundering skies and flambéing entire villages. And since then, the idea of their existence had made its way through the centuries up to today via tongue, papyrus, and celluloid.

He told her about the hours spent at his drafting table, and then the weeks in actual construction making certain that his "boys" would be completely different from the killer-breath monstrosities that had fueled those flickering campfire fables so many years ago. He had designed his dragons standing up rather than down on all fours because he had wanted them to be characters for the kids to make pals with and call their own rather than heinous brooding beasts to scare the water right out of them in the middle of the night. That was something Gabe's boss, Malcolm Conet, had agreed with wholeheartedly. Then he told Kate about Betty Valieri and how she had changed everything. How Gabe had bowed to her terms, and now the Dragons Three were what they were.

Wide-eyed, Kate said the whole thing was "just simply, utterly, unbelievably awesome" —or something to that effect. And Gabe thought she was just interested in his lean, tan body. Or something to that effect.

The steel-blue Z-28 lovingly embraced the street as it swung around, did a neat U-turn, and braked parallel to the sidewalk in front of the Holden house. The street was dark and tucked in for the night.

At twenty after nine the tiny restaurant had been closing and Kate had insisted she'd drive Gabe home. There'd been no arm twisting involved whatsoever. She had her older brother's car and handled the purring beast like a pro.

She tossed it into park and turned to Gabe, laying her right arm across the back of the seat. Gabe had planned on putting *his* arm there but just wasn't swift enough. He could have smoothly laid one arm on top of hers but decided against it, leaving his hands folded like a napkin in his lap. He felt incredibly awkward. In truth, he couldn't help feeling how much he was playing the girl's role and Kate was playing the guy's. Roxy Music trickled to the front from the back-seat speakers.

"I had a wunnerful time." Kate smiled.

"Wunnerful place," Gabe said, gesturing toward her.

"Hey, what's a wunnerful place without some wunnerful company?" she said.

"Wunnerful."

"Wunnerful."

They had run plumb out of "wunnerfuls" and now it was all up to Gabe to think of something original to say to finish the evening off nicely. But Gabe didn't feel extremely original at the moment, so without much thought, he came up with: "You wanna come in for a nightcap?"

(Oh! Oh, now *that* was original! What's next, Gabe? "Hey, babe, come on up to the bedroom and I'll show you my etchings of Maurice the Hossenfeffer"? *That* oughta cinch it.)

Gabe wished the words would just crawl back down his throat, but it was too late.

"A distinct idiot, moron, jerk, scuzzoid feeling just went through me," Gabe said, shaking his head.

Kate cracked up. Gabe managed to laugh along with her.

"No, I've got to get home and back into my coffin," she said, truly sorry. "I haven't been getting to sleep until after midnight all this week, and I've got to get into some heavy-duty z's, y'know? Anyway, I've got to get the car back to Nigel. I think he had somewhere to go toni—"

"No," Gabe said, from out of nowhere.

Kate's eyebrows jumped. She couldn't tell if Gabe was serious.

(You're in it now, guy.)

"Come. Come with me to the far lands of Baghdad," Gabe said, putting on an accent that required fastening the tongue to the roof of the mouth. He didn't quite know why he'd said that line, but he desperately hoped she would laugh, ending the evening off on a good note. She didn't laugh but did something else, totally unexpected. She went along with it.

She leaned forward and took his hands in hers. Gabe inhaled the perfume of her hair. She gazed deeply into his face with those punishing chocolate eyes of hers.

"Oh, if only I could," she said. Her voice was filled with just the right amount of despair. "That's what I want more than anything in the world, but . . . it could never be."

Obviously, the girl had seen the same golden oldie once.

"Of course it can," Gabe said earnestly.

"But my father would find us wherever we went. He has forbidden me to . . . to even *speak* to you. If he finds me now . . . I don't know *what* he'd do," she breathed fearfully.

"But he doesn't know that . . . that I am . . . I am a *prince*. Before I was the Thief of Baghdad—"

"It doesn't matter," she said, dejected.

Gabe held her hands tighter in the true dramatic fashion.

"Come. Come with me," he urged. "Come with me right now . . . *to the ends of the earth.*"

Whereupon, she took Gabe's face in her hands and pressed her open strawberry mouth to his. Ah, bliss.

Thirty-five minutes later Gabe unlocked the front door and came in with his ten-speed. The big house was filled with icy darkness. He turned the bike over on its back and dropped the chain along with the brand-new tires he had picked up at the bike shop. He took off his khaki jacket and put on his bulky Kangaroo jacket from the foyer closet.

He went over to the family room and switched on the radio on the immense stereo system. A classical station.

In the kitchen, he made a double-decker roast beef sandwich beside the sink. He went back into the living room, mouth stuffed with sandwich, a roll of newspapers under his arm. He slipped the papers under the bicycle and changed the tires, oiled the chain, and cleaned all the joints and hidden angles of the frame.

Finished, he pushed himself up, walked over to the back door, and slid it open. He felt the night breeze in his eyes. He stepped out onto the veranda and plopped down on one of the frayed lawn chairs.

Gabe smiled openly, thinking about Kate. They had made a plan to meet again tomorrow. She had another eating place in mind. This time it was of the Chinese persuasion, her treat. And afterward they would catch a Sunday midnight showing of *The Road Warrior* at the Palace 33.

Pushing his hair back, he looked at Tyler's wading pool, the water's surface covered with floating dead coffee-colored leaves, a Hershey bar wrapper, and a potato chip bag. He decided he'd clean it out tomorrow, for sure.

And they were there. The sparrows. Gabe laughed loudly, stopped, and laughed again, but not so loudly this time.

"Yo, guys! Wanna come in for a beer? Nobody's home and we can really get plowed. Wattaya say?"

Not much.

They just sat there and stared, clustered on the fence top at the end of the yard. They didn't change places, peck at each other, or take off. Just like all week, they just . . . stared. Weird.

Once more the head-whispers returned, but this time they had been slightly clarified. This time he could almost feel it in the air. A subtle aura, a pale sensation of imminence, something coming up soon, something of a cryptic nature.

Groaning out loud, he put his arms behind his head. He was getting very tired of these morbid musings of his. He wondered if normal people ever had these thoughts. He wondered where this menacing thinking originated. He wondered what these bedeviling notions signified. He wondered if he was okay.

He stared back stupidly at the group of dark sparrows for a while longer, then went inside, sliding the door shut with a whack. He would never see those little birds ever again.

Gabe flicked off the switches of the stereo system in the family room and went back to the kitchen. He had downed the roast beef sandwich, but his hunger was still not satiated. He went on a snack hunt.

Humming away, he inspected the pantry up and down. A folded bag of Peek Freans chocolate digestive cookies caught his fancy, along with a net sack with a few walnuts huddled together in the bottom. He tossed them onto the counter. He found the nutcracker with one hand and took Dad's monogrammed beer mug down from the cupboard with the other. He whipped

109

open the refrigerator door, lifted a sloshing carton of milk, and filled Dad's mug to the rim, then snatched a couple of oranges.

With the load cradled in his arms, Gabe shuffled into the living room. He seated himself in the deep soft chair and put the mug of milk and his feet on the coffee table. Giving an unending yawn, he reached for the remote control and turned on the TV. The screen flickered and quickly lit up with images. He increased the volume.

". . . kiss me, Wilfred."

"Don't do it, Willie," Gabe said.

Click.

"—y'all c'n clap now, ah'm finished."

Click.

"—ost this much sleep, a person such as yourself would become delirious—"

Click.

"—nd we'll be right back with even more of Slim Whitman's three-hour Thanksgiving special in San Hoi—"

"Gag."

Click.

"—coming to you at this hour of the day to share with you, step by step, how to convert a wheelchair into a dune bug—"

Click.

"—inhale deeply, now, Mrs. Nobooboo. We're about to externalize your innermost thoughts—"

Click.

"—elieve it! You can be ordained in a mere nine weeks! Just send—"

Click.

"—thrill once more to the sounds of Carlos

Brudinskipo, renowned master of the Jew's harp and power saw—"

Click.

". . . Kiss me again, Wilfred."

Nearing an hour later, Gabe was still at it. He was tired, but not enough to go to sleep. He had changed back to channel 6 and found *Coma* was on for the umpty-umpth time. His left leg was hanging over the arm of the chair and he was spinning the rear wheel on his ten-speed with the toe of his Nike runner.

He looked around. The mug was almost empty, the cookie bag was crumpled into a little ball, and the orange rinds had nothing to protect anymore. The walnut sack was stuffed down the inside of the chair. He pulled it out and shook it, looking for a lone survivor, and discovered one intact walnut among the shucks. He wedged it between the teeth of the nutcracker and began the kill.

Gabe increased the compression ever so slightly, but the nut showed no sign of breaking. He reached out for the mug and took a drink of milk.

Gabe tightened his grip around the nutcracker. It reminded him of a hand-exercise tool some executive might use sitting behind his desk. Or her desk. Maybe Valieri uses one. Yeah, that would be just like her. He could see it. Her crooked, bloodless, skeletal hand crushing, crushing. Gabe's hand began to show tension, straining. The nut wasn't breaking.

The light from the television danced on his face, making his moist eyes twinkle.

His fingers were rigidly clutched now, squeez-

ing down on the walnut between the jaws of the
nutcracker, squeezing, squeezing . . .
(Just)
squeezing . . .
(like)
squeezing . . .
(her!)
squeeeeeeeeEEEEE*EEE*-CRACKKTCH!
Crushed, the walnut flew apart in big pieces.
Then the heavy hand grabbed his shoulder
from behind.
And Gabe's world flew apart in big pieces.
He jackknifed headfirst over the coffee table
and whirled.
He was instantly ready for, ready for—
—not this. Not this.
"Hello, Daddy. It's time to play."

Seven

All was sight.

There was nothing else.

There was no beginning. There was no end.

There was nothing else.

There was no sound. Not any feeling.

There was nothing else.

All was sight.

Novocain shot through Gabe's hollow arms and legs. He had pushed himself back, shriveling, against the screen of the television set. He was blocking the light, obscuring his vision of the figures in front of him. But he didn't need the light.

(. . . . . . .)

Then a lamp was turned on. There. Deep down, far below the surface, Gabe had known who it was all along. Oh, yes, but he had refused any articulate thought of it. Refused the idea of . . . it. But that didn't lessen the raw terror that pierced his heart again and again. He was awed. This should not be.

(. . . . . . .)

York, Sid, and Hubub stood in a rough semicircle, their chests rising and falling with their furnace breathing. They showed teeth.

Gabe blinked. Again, again, again.

His hobby was alive and had surrounded him.
(. . . . . . .)

Somewhere, sometime in one's life, one comes face-to-face—or in Gabe's case, face-to-face-to-face-to-face—with something that actually *pushes* the brain to believe. It shoves and forces and drives the stubborn mind to accept whatever it is as something real and treat it as so.

Gabe was trying his very best, but his very best wasn't even close. His mind was a fluttering blank sheet of paper. He could not accept this. It should not be.

The room was full of long shadows that lay on the carpet and leaned up against the walls. The muscles on Dragons Three looked even larger now, bloated. Their shirts were gone, but they still had the crumpled shorts Gabe had picked out for them.

Hubub plopped down and made himself comfortable in the love seat. Gabe thought he heard him giggle. Sid was behind the big chair Gabe had been sitting in, his big hands on the back. York strode over to the back door, hands behind him, and looked out into the frigid darkness. He turned, toward the pale, upturned face of Gabe.

"A little . . . jumpy, aren't we, Father?" His voice was deep and rich. The dragon approached, leaned down leisurely, and with the heels of his brawny hands cupped under Gabe's jawline, he raised Gabe to his feet, then let him go. Gabe fell back on the TV set for support, his left hand coming into contact with something— the beer mug. He still had it. Gabe gripped the handle in his white fist, as if he were planning to—

Hubub giggled. York came closer. Gabe looked

114

into his bestial face. The face *he* had given him.
The eyes blinked and glittered. They were so
alive. The nostrils dilated, and Gabe could feel
the hot air rush out of them. The rims of his
mouth glistened with saliva.

(. . . saliva)

He could not accept this.

"You're not taking this well, Father," York
said. It was almost a purr.

Hubub chuckled.

"Questions, hmm?"

Gabe almost nodded, his eyes wide and
glassy.

*"Yesss, questions to be asked . . . to be an-
swered."* The dragon's words came tonelessly,
as if it had just learned to speak. *"You don't believe what you see with your own eyes."*

Gabe almost nodded again. York gave a long
sigh. His hot breath had a vile odor to it. It nau-
seated Gabe.

*"Doesn't matter. All that matters now is . . .
we are here."*

(They are here. . . .)

"We live."

(They live. . . .)

*"The house . . . it is ours now. We have
waited."*

(It is theirs now . . . ?)

"You want to know . . . why."

This time Gabe did nod. The laugh gathered
somewhere in the far reaches of the dragon's
throat and stayed there, a steady rumbling inside his shell. The rich suppressed laughter
spread from dragon to dragon until the unearthly sound pervaded the living room and
seemed to push against the walls. It was secre-

tive, frightening, anticipatory laughter. Then it dwindled to the low sniggerings of Hubub. Then it stopped.

York stepped even closer to Gabe, nailing the boy's eyes mercilessly with his own. For one harrowing instant he thought he was about to get his face barbecued. The fire never came.

"You are our father. You brought us here. We gave you the chance . . . the warnings. Go with your family. You didn't listen to us."

"No, Daddy didn't listen to us," Hubub said with a tune.

"Does the daddy ever listen to his children?" Sid hissed humorlessly.

York's stare did not waver from Gabe's face.

"Time. Our time has come."

"High time," Sid sneered.

Gabe's grip on the mug handle tightened.

"You have to . . . " York tensed. *". . . leave. You would stand in the way of it."*

Gabe's eyebrows flicked, quizzical.

"The surge, Father. Ours." Parched pause. *"We're taking advantage of the situation."*

Gabe thought he heard Hubub smack his lips together. Hot blood was roaring in his ears. York inhaled and spoke. Deadpan finality.

"Our time has come. Your time has passed. The house is ours. We have waited. We gave you the cha—"

GUNCH!!

Gabe's fist had come around in a blurred sweep with the beer mug. There was the awful intimate sound of breaking teeth and a sharp shocked yip from York. Gabe bolted for the stairs.

His ten-speed, balanced on its back, was between Sid and Hubub. Gabe charged low past Sid, pulling the bike down hard. That slowed Sid up a precious instant, but the huge Hubub was up and grabbing for Gabe's back as he reached the stairs.

Just as Gabe hit the first step, he seemed to go into slow motion, taking cartoon leaps and bounds. From no place, a sweet little tune popped into his head.

(Tik-tok-tik-tok. The mouse ran up the . . .)

The stairs were a ladder. Gabe was pushing himself off the smooth walls, scrambling up, up! There were thundering yells behind him, ringing off the walls, and Hubub was almost on him, laughing.

(tik-tok-tik-tok)

Gabe had gotten halfway up the ladder. He knew that because he had passed the photograph of Mom's parents. Then, horribly, Gabe felt his Kangaroo jacket being grabbed from behind.

(Not gonna make it.)

Hubub had him. Gabe's left hand went to his zipper and yanked, but he was already being pulled to a stop. He had to get it off!

(tika-toka-tika-toka)

ZZZIIP

He got it off and Hubub had a handful of jacket. Gabe fell forward, and he couldn't feel stairs anymore. He was at the top! Then he screamed. His foot was fire. He looked back down and saw Hubub had his foot in his jaws, chomping, chomping.

Gabe kicked savagely at the dragon's head, again and again until he tore his foot free. He

117

stamped down with his other foot, sending Hubub back, how far he didn't know.

(tika-toka-tika-toka)

Gabe raked at the shag carpet with his finger-nails, pulling himself up into the darkness. He crawled toward his room, but the door was closed. All of a sudden he felt drained. He couldn't get up. And he couldn't reach his door-knob.

(Gaining on me.)

He knew York and Sid would be on him any time now, clawing, biting, ripping the pink flesh from him.

(Please, oh please, let me make it, I gotta.)

Then Gabe found he was lying on his belly halfway inside Mom and Dad's bedroom. He clutched at the doorframe and dragged himself in all the way. He dared a look over his shoulder, and Sid's snarling face appeared at the top of the stairs, eyes aflame.

"Daddeeeeeeeeeeeeeeeee!" the thing screamed, coming at him.

Gabe banged the door shut, locked it. There was a second of silence, then the door was smashed against from the outside.

Gabe plastered himself against the door, his whole body quaking with the beating of his heart. Hot salty tears spilled down his face, into his open mouth.

"Holy holy holy holy holy holy holy holy holy holy g- holy g- holy God holy God. OH MY . . . GOD!!!" Gabe shrieked through clenched teeth. The door was smashed again, and Gabe was thrown forward onto his hands.

(No, I don't believe any of this, not this, no. I DON'T BELIEVE ANY OF THIS.)

He was a quivering, blubbering mess now. The hot blood racing in his head was deafening. Supper, the double-decker roast beef sandwich, the oranges and cookies, were boiling inside him. Gabe shut his eyes, his head spinning.

There were no more smashings against the bedroom door. Gabe mashed his right ear against it. He could hear faint grunts and murmurings. Then laughter. He guessed they were all up there now. There was the sound of a door opening . . . then closing. Then, thumpings. One of them going down the stairs. He wiped his wet face with both hands. He listened again. Nothing. Then . . .

"Daddeeee, come out and playyy. Oh, won't you come outside, Daddy? We want to play with you. Come outside and play. We've been waiting alllll day long for you to come home." It was a vicious hiss. Sid. He was right up against the other side of the door.

Abruptly there was a barrage of noise. The floor throbbed with it. High-energy rock music. The stereo downstairs had been turned on and turned up. Loud.

Gabe bit down on all ten fingers, shivering. His eyes shifted crazily. He began to giggle.

"What . . . what's . . . what's happening here? To me? Whaaaaaaat?"

(Crazy. Crazy, that it? Is this what it's like? Crazy?)

He was really starting to lose it. He couldn't decide whether to turn on the big light in the room or not. He left it off. He moved over to the doors that led out to a small porch overlooking the backyard. He unlocked the glass door and slid it open. He looked over. There was no way he could make a getaway. Too far down. Too far.

Hobbling from his aching ankle, he lugged Dad's rolltop desk in front of the door, then squatted in the far corner of the room, holding his stomach. He stared blankly at the blocked door.

The smashings on the door started again, and Gabe knew this time they weren't going to stop until they got in. He was standing now, knees bent, fists clenched together against his pelvis. His eyes darted around, looking, looking. He scrambled toward the oak dresser, hot knives stabbing his ankle and up into his calf, and yanked open the top drawer. He hurled out pieces of clothing furiously, praying that Tyler had put it back. The drawer was so deep.

(Come on, Tyler, come on. Come on, don't do this to me.)

The bedroom door was snapping right off its hinges.

Then Gabe felt it in the far right corner. Yes! There it was, snug against a box of ammo.

(I love ya, kid.)

He grabbed Dad's .38 pistol, flipped out the cylinder. He had something now. He had cold power. He dumped the little box of ammunition upside down on the dresser top. Bullets rolled everywhere. His fingers were icy and next to useless.

A green fist punched through the door.

Gabe fumbled with the bullets, flicking them into their chambers. Wide-eyed, he limped over to the open porch door. He had never considered suicide, but if the bullets couldn't stop the dragons, he'd rather take a flying leap than be grabbed and eaten alive by those monsters.

(My . . . boys . . . ?)

He stood at the entrance to the porch. Frigid winds whipped in, making his teeth click together. A shiver rose inside him. He held the hunk of jet steel in both hands, trying to find the best grip.

Dad had purchased the weapon a little over a year ago and had taken Gabe to a shooting range twice. Gabe had always scored higher than Dad at the range, but he'd never thought much of it. Now, when he really needed it, he couldn't even hold the blasted thing right.

ch-ch-k-krraackshk

(Sweet Jesus, help.)

A tiny moan came up with his breath.

The door was buckling open, green claws clutching, jostling Dad's desk. They would be in the room in seconds. He could see their burning eyes.

The bed was between Gabe and the doorway. That would give him time to aim and get off a good one, maybe two. Gabe wanted to shoot and shoot and shoot some more, but he waited. He had to.

For one twinkling moment he felt an all-consuming impulse to give up. Just throw the gun away, fall to the floor, curl up in a little ball and just give up.

ch-K-KOOOOOMM! The desk came crashing down and the door erupted into flying chunks. The high-energy rock music filled the room. His guts constricted.

(I don't want this. I DON'T WANT THIS.)

Bellowing victoriously, Hubub bore down on

Gabe, arms outstretched, froth streaming from his open mouth. And he had something in his big hands. A steak knife and fork. He kept on coming even when Gabe jerked up the shiny .38.

He tugged the trigger back.

K-CHOW!

White-eyed, Gabe watched the slug go awry and whack into the plasterboard of the far wall. The dragon did not stop.

K-CHOW!

The second slug nicked Hubub's shoulder. Pieces of his hide flew. The dragon did not stop. Gabe gave a little cry.

K-CHOW!

The third slug punched through Hubub's flaming left eye and tore into his skull. The dragon stopped. His victorious roar yanked up to an unearthly screeching noise. He clutched his face and plunged to the floor, rolling, bucking. The scene horrified Gabe but he didn't have long because Sid was coming up fast.

(Madness . . .)

There was no time to think, none at all. It was all go-go-go.

The explosions from the pistol had numbed his hands and he was fumbling again. Sid sailed low over the bed. The gun seemed to have taken on weight, and Gabe couldn't get it up fast enough. The dragon hit him like a prairie freight train, slamming the wind out of him and picking him off his feet.

They were going over. Over the railing of the porch and into the cold clear air. Gabe reached out for the railing, missed, but grabbed hold of the edge of the porch itself.

So had Sid.

"Guh!" His arms were nearly wrenched right out of their sockets and everything felt ripped, but he had grabbed hold.

The two of them hung there, chests heaving. Gabe held on with both hands, the .38 still on his right index finger. He looked over at Sid, who looked back with seething hatred in his eyes. Cool droplets began to sprinkle.

Shutting out the unending drop beneath him, Gabe tried to gain a better grip on the wet porch. He saw he was going to have to do something fast because Sid was rapidly making his move. The beast had dropped to one powerful arm and was swiping at Gabe with the other one. Sid tried again and again, but Gabe kept pivoting his head, just beyond his grasp.

Sid started to slide over, coming closer, closer. Gabe felt warm tears well up in his eyes.

(Not fair, it's not fair.)

Sid had all the triceps and biceps and he could stay up there all night, but Gabe only had thin arms and he was already slipping. He started to cry out in great heavy sobs.

Sid was very close now. The dragon snapped his teeth together with a resonant chomp and dropped easily to one arm again. This was his last swipe and Gabe's very last chance.

"I love you, Daddy."

Visibly relishing this, Sid reached out for his prize. The eyeballs. The whimpering boy dropped to one arm also and brought the pistol up, but his vision was blurred by the rain. Sid had him. The weapon thundered and shook itself free from Gabe's white fingers. He shut his streaming eyes, swinging by one arm, waiting for Sid to, for Sid to . . .

He opened his eyes. Sid was gone. Gabe gaped downward. He could make out the monster lying sprawled on the backyard lawn, his left leg tucked under him. There was a black hole bang in the center of his chest.

Gabe brought his free hand up and grabbed the porch. With racking efforts, he hauled himself up halfway and wedged one knee between the railings. He stood unsteadily on the rim and twisted over, safe. He giggled hysterically. It was a shrill sound. He swallowed and something came up, tart, burning in his throat. He opened his mouth, drank in the pellets of rain, then looked back down again. He couldn't spot the .38.

Arms crossed across his chest, he turned and went slowly through the bedroom, stepping around the immobile form of Hubub. Dad's desk was thrust aside, the roll cover crushed. The drawers had fallen out, the contents scattered. Pieces of the busted door crunched under his feet. The music from the family room downstairs rocked on, pummeling his brain. Trembling openly, he balanced all his weight on his good foot and leaned against the doorframe.

Then he went wooden, staring down the hallway at a line of light underneath the closed door of his bedroom.

"York."

Gabe backed up rigidly into Mom and Dad's bedroom. Petrified, he was expecting York to come storming down the hallway any second. And this time Gabe didn't have a door. He didn't have a gun. He needed something and he needed it pronto. His eyes fell on Dad's overturned desk and its spilled contents. Keeping a

124

...tery watch on the black mine shaft of the hall-way, Gabe kneeled on the carpet. He sifted through the endless pencils, pens, hotel match-books, junk, junk, and even more junk until he found it. Its original luster was gone and the blade was bent slightly at an angle, but it still held a keen point and that was damn straight enough. Gabe clenched the stainless steel letter opener in both hands and left the bedroom.

Pressing himself up against the right wall, he shuffled heavily down the hallway. The rock music increased sharply as he neared the top of the stairs. He halted, holding the letter opener against his sternum, the point piercing the air. His eyes flitted back and forth. No sign of York.

(Don't come out, come out, wherever you are. . . .)

He looked anxiously at his closed bed-room door and the filament of milky light that showed beneath it. But, if York *was* in there—

(What is he doing?)

He jettisoned the curiosity. It didn't matter. All that mattered was getting down the stairs and out of this live-in nightmare. The stairs, the stairs were everything. He started for them, but then paused. His eyes went unhappily to his door.

He *had* to know.

(What is he doing in there?)

Something of such importance that he would let Daddy get away? He had to know. It became a necessity.

Standing there, he felt coldly exposed. He tightened his grip on the letter opener. It was his only security in the world at the moment.

He stepped toward his door.

125

He raised his left hand to the copper-colored knob. The act felt genuinely weird. Foreign. His twitching fingers wavered, then closed around the knob.

And that's when the rock music died.

Silence. He remained stationary, rooted where he was. His eyes flicked to the stairs, and then his head reluctantly followed suit. He glared fearfully down into the darkness.

The stereo was silent. It had been turned off. Or maybe it was a cassette tape and it had finished. Yeah, it was a tape, and it had ended.

(Right in the middle of a song?)

He buttoned down an insane, giggling urge to scream.

He held his position, as if waiting for York to come crawling up the stairs, coming for him step by step by . . . Gabe took the chance and, in one brisk movement, twisted the knob, swiveled inside, banged the door shut, and locked it. He brought the blade up high and his mouth dropped open.

His room was cleared. Everything!—his bed, dresser, desk, bookcase, drafting table—had all been brutally shoveled into his closet.

It was quiet in the room. A dusty quiet. The only light came from his Ford Model A desk lamp. It was on the floor where his desk had been. The shade had been knocked off. The naked bulb created an eerie light.

Gabe inhaled. The room smelled. It smelled . . . old. As if it had been here for a very long time. And it felt . . . it felt cold and dark, almost like a cave or a . . . lair.

Parallel with the far wall where his bed had been was the ironing board. And it had an occu-

126

pant, although covered with a white sheet from his bed. Sitting on the floor to the right of the board were the boxes of dragon supplies. The tops were flipped open and the materials inside had been mixed around, as if someone had just been using them. Smartly tacked to the wall were the two full-scale diagrams of the original Holden Dragon. And over all this was the word, crudely, almost savagely scratched. No, not scratched but *furrowed* through Gabe's outer space mural and into the wall.

SURGE

(Oh . . . God . . . no.)

Silvery ice water laced through Gabe, beginning at his scalp, running down his bare arms, speeding to his legs. He was numb, heavy.

A peeling back of paper in his mind. Four tight walls of an office. The face of an old woman. A dripping smile. Valieri. The Surge, Gabe. The Surge.

His eyelids fluttered as if trying to clear away the image before him. But it was still there, dug into the wall.

His eyes rolled down until they fixed on the still, shrouded shape on the ironing board.

He did *not* want to see what was under that sheet.

Running started to sound like a sterling, class A-1 idea again. He had seen enough.

No, he hadn't seen enough. It will never be enough. Not until he shoots the works. Not until he goes all the way with this. Not until he sees under that sheet.

Not that he didn't already know. Oh, yes, the boy was wise the moment he saw the ironing board set up against the wall. He knew. It was the act of confirmation that terrified him. It *terrified* him.

Gabe's feet were dead slabs of beef inside his Nikes, weighing down his legs. He lifted them off the carpet and closed in. Shifting the letter opener to his left hand, he rubbed his clammy palm on his leg and switched the opener back to his right hand.

Eyes swelling in their sockets, he raised his left arm and pinched the top corner of the sheet between his fingertips. His heart was wham-wham-whamming away inside his neck and ears, filling the small room with a blunt drumbeat, picking up tempo. Nostrils flaring, he brought up the steel letter opener in a quavering fist, took a firmer grip on the sheet, and yanked it back, revealing . . .

Gabe's breath quit in his chest.

The ice water lacing through his veins froze.

Laid out neatly, all four limbs aligned with the edges of the board, was the body of a partially constructed dragon. The complete fiberglass skeleton was accurately positioned on the pad. The latex hide was stitched to both legs and the right side of the torso, leaving the left exposed. This gave it the appearance of a dissected cadaver. The left side of the fiendish face was also bared, but the wicked ruby eyeballs were already secured in their sockets. It was a death's head, glowering, smiling horridly up at him.

128

Gabe's flesh was alive. His eyes darted up and down the form. He willed himself back from the sight.

(What . . . are they planning on . . . doing? WHAT ARE THEY PLANNING ON DOING?)

His eyes studied the unfinished dragon. There was something about it, something vague. For one thing, it didn't have the robust build of the other three dragons. He was sure of it. Or was he? After all he had seen tonight, what on this spinning earth *could* he be sure of?

No, there *was* something undeniably different about this dragon. Something about the contour of the frame. It was rounded, curved, giving the dragon an odd aspect—trim, smooth, even soft. It was beginning to look, in every sense of the word, extremely and frighteningly . . . *feminine*.

Gabe found this deeply distressing.

He wobbled back a step, two, three, grimacing. Denial. Denial became horror. Horror rapidly became repulsion.

Mental traffic accelerated: ideas, beliefs, sentiments rampantly intersected one another.

Surge

(Uh-uh, no way, this is wrong, all wrong. No, can't happen, no. I—I didn't.)

SUrge

(No, no chance. A—a female. Craziness. Toys, just toys. They couldn't.)

SURge

(Please, please, it's not true, not real. Nothing's real, not this.)

SURGe

(No, no! Impossible, impossible. They're just toys. NonononononoNO.)

SURGE

"No! No way! That's impossible! They can't! They CAN'T!"

Gabe's right leg snapped up, powerfully slicing through the air and taking the ironing board with it. The incomplete dragon arched, sailing freely, until it struck the left wall and shattered, both arms and the right leg breaking off and falling away. The rest of it crumbled to the floor as the ironing board smashed back down to earth, clattering still. And all was dusty quiet in the room again.

Looking like a newcomer to the scene, Gabe stood there, blinking like a child. Breath coming and going laboriously, he moistened the roof of his mouth. Fists still clenched, he wearily took in the mess. He looked down solemnly at the ruined dragon propped up against the wall, pinned beneath the ironing board.

He shouldn't have kicked it. It was wrong. It *felt* wrong. It felt . . .

(Insane.)

After all, it *was* just a toy, remember? A lifeless, inanimate thing.

(After all, after all . . .)

The demolished dragon's grimacing head was tilted to the left, gazing past Gabe, contemplating the ceiling, as if it were making eye contact with, with . . .

(A mate.)

A low liquid snarling behind him building into rage.

Gabe pirouetted crazily, eyes up, and everything clicked together in his brain.

130

*York—wedged up in the far corner of the
ceiling—all this time—flying at me!*

Gabe ducked, all the way to the carpeted
floor.

He felt the plunging dragon just clear his
head and heard the crushing wallop when he hit
the wall behind him and fell to the floor, thrash-
ing.

Gabe lunged for the door, for the knob, for his
life.

He clutched at the knob, but something was
wrong. He couldn't grab the knob in his hand,
nothing was working, the icy fingers were not
his and he, he couldn't . . .

(GetoutgetoutgetOUT.)

. . . get the knob in his fingers. His nails were
scratching flimsily at the wood around the knob
and he couldn't get any kind of grip on it and
here comes York!

He clapped the knob between both palms and
twisted, dropping the letter opener in the frenzied process. No time, no time, He spilled out of
the door opening, into the black hallway, and
made for the stairs. He whipped a look back to
see if—but the dragon was *right there!*

Howling, York slammed into him full throt-
tle. Gabe caught the monstrosity in his arms,
and for one second, the two figures were air-
borne. Fused together, they crashed violently
down the stairs, twisting and bouncing all the
way to the bottom.

Still connected, they ricocheted off a wall and
for a moment were doing the polka. The dragon's vile breath was so hot and sweet it stuck to
Gabe's face.

York's face was now a coiling, snorting horror. It wasn't York anymore. Not Gabe's York. Straining to hold the dragon back with both hands, Gabe instantly realized it *wasn't* his York because his York was latex and foam and fiberglass. What he felt now was flesh; what he felt now was muscle, what he felt now was *bone*.

Gabe shrieked. York had a lion's share of his arm in his slavering mouth and it felt as if the limb had already been ripped off.

It felt like a picket fence was burrowing into him, shredding him, peppering the side of his face with his blood. His hot blood. And it hurt, it *hurt*, it hurrr— Gabe pounded frantically on the side of the monster's head, lost his balance, and both of them toppled heavily into the living room.

Gabe kicked out hard, heel first, at York's side, sending him farther into the room. Gabe got up on one knee. A table lamp was in front of his face. In one movement, he tore the plug from the wall and swung the lamp down on York's skull. The monster hit the floor, but the lamp bounced off the dragon's head and out of Gabe's grip, rolling away. And now the green beast was rising and Gabe was falling, sucking in air. He reached back blindly for something to pull himself up with and the back of his hand banged on a pole. The ten-speed.

He scrambled maniacally back and took hold of the freshly oiled bicycle chain laid out on the newspaper in a perfect oval.

York was up on all fours now, looking larger than life. Gabe pitched forward mindlessly onto the dragon's massive back, looping the chain around his telephone-pole neck. Gabe snapped back, leaning with his full weight. The harmless bike chain was now a steel garrote.

Jumping to his feet, York clutched at the chain around his throat, trying to work his hooked claws under it, but it was no good. The thin belt of metal was secured, almost a piece of him. He whipped his huge head from side to side like an enraged bull, slicing at the air with his clicking talons.

Gabe could feel the dragon's immense back muscles bunch up beneath his coarse pebbled hide, and in a shuddering eruption of movement, York catapulted headlong through the back door, smashing the glass, and headed across the veranda into the backyard. But Gabe hung on.

With the choking load on his back, York stumbled and slipped on the drenched grass. His jagged mouth gaped open, his breath came out in long grating wheezes. The chain was doing it.

This was it. This was for keeps and Daddy wasn't letting up.

Eyes bulging, the monster went berserk.

York hurled himself down violently onto the sodden ground. All Gabe could do was hold on to the bike chain with his bloody fingers. The sharp edges of the links bit through the soft flesh of his hands.

The two figures rolled over and over through Mom's flower bed, slashing and shredding the delicate plants. York struggled to his feet, but then the dragon started reeling backward and tumbled into freezing water.

They had crashed into Tyler's Mr. Turtle pool. The kiddie pool was instantly filled with a frenzy of slashing, lashing, grappling fury. Coughing and sputtering, Gabe hectically maneuvered himself up onto the front of the floundering dragon, twisting the chain around his tree-trunk neck, wrenching it taut. He glared down into the monster's writhing face. The eyes were ruby ice. The horrible mouth, filled with jagged teeth, snapped again and again beneath the filthy water. There were no bubbles. Gabe almost smiled.

(Winning . . . I'm winning.)

Then the brawny, knuckled hand broke the surface of the water. Gabe saw it coming, but there wasn't thing one he could do to stop it. Massive fingers spread and closed around the boy's pulsing jugular.

York, the firstborn, was unstoppable. The fingers were steel bars and the arm behind it was an iron beam.

Gabe could feel the white-hot pointed claws pierce the flesh of his neck. His whole being wailed at him to let go of the bicycle chain and rip the killing hand away, but he couldn't do that. He wouldn't have a chance then.

(Let go of the chain.)

He couldn't breathe now. York had cut off his air. He jerked the chain tighter.

(Let GO of the CHAIN.)

His mouth opened to gag. He didn't know how much more of this agony he could take. He tasted blood in the bottom of his mouth.

(LET GO OF THE CHAIN.)

He stared down at his fingers. The blood was mixing with the oil on the chain. Then he noticed the chain wasn't tight anymore. It had slipped through his greased fingers. It was back to harmless slack. Frantic, he gripped the links, pulling them taut again, but they were slick with oil and blood. Gabe made another effort but slip, slip, slip.

Then he stopped trying. He blinked, eyebrows wrinkling.

The mighty York wasn't struggling anymore. No movement to him at all. He was stiff. The decaying cover of coffee-colored leaves floating on the surface of the water had already closed in around his head.

Gabe let go of the chain. His trembling hands went up to the claws, still around his narrow neck. He bent the powerful fingers back and dropped the limb.

Gabe looked down at the rigid, silent form of York, then hobbled away from the wading pool, heading for the house. He was battered, bloody, and coated in clumps of mud.

He gazed down at the fallen form of Sid, and something shiny caught his eye. Dad's .38 pistol. With many pains, Gabe bent down to pick up the weapon from the grass. He tottered over to the veranda and took the steps like an old man. Hunched over, he limped sluggishly across the veranda and stepped into the muggy warmth of the house. A frigid gust of rain sprayed over him from behind.

Gabe turned off the television and stood in the middle of the living room. There was silence. Nothing else. All was still. He touched his wounds. They were electric hot. But the horror wasn't there anymore. He had come through it and he had survived.

Then, behind him, he heard the worst thing of his life.

"Father?"

York's hulking frame filled the backyard entrance. His eyes were sizzling blades. He was alive.

"Time, Father. It's time." The words were acid.

(No, please . . . stop, please. . . .)

He was alive and he was unstoppable and he was coming for Daddy. And then, so was Sid, with the black hole bang in the center of his chest. And Hubub, with the three slugs in his face, was lumbering down the stairs, chuckling. And he had his steak knife and fork again.

Gabe tried to back away, but they had him surrounded. York was coming for Gabe's jugular and Sid was coming for his eyes. And Hubub was coming for his golden-fried ankle.

Gabe curled his slick fingers around the handle and brought the pistol up, straight-armed. He took the best aim he had ever taken because he knew it was all he had the strength to do. A small muscle twitched in Gabe's finger and he gently, almost serenely, squeezed the trigger. The gun exploded. York careened back with it, crashing into Sid, both of them toppling into Dad's recliner.

Gabe reeled back, tripping over his ten-speed, and Hubub was on him, knife and fork at the ready. The huge dragon took the last bullet in the mouth and flailed backward.

Gabe pulled himself up, clutching at the drapes across the bay window. But York was still alive and kicking and so was Sid and they were grasping and tearing at him from the floor. He brought Dad's gun down on their heads, again, again, fighting savagely, but the room was slipping upward and he was tipping over, only one hand left on the drapes. And then he started to whimper because he could see Hubub crawling toward him and thick white froth was bubbling over and he had his cutlery again and he was laughing loud and Gabe's drumstick legs were being eaten alive and the lizards the world over were roaring and he could see Saint George shaking his head and he was screaming for Mommy and losing his head and being clawed and ripped and grabbed and pulled all the way down, down. . . .

And then the front door opened and the Holdens walked in and all things stopped dead on a tightwire.

Panting hoarsely, Gabriel turned his bloody, bone-white face to the foyer. His eyes were round and barren. A wet shank of hair hung down over one eye, obstructing his view. Everything was a silvery-blue smear of a brush. Then the picture came together and it gradually sank into Gabe just who they were.

His family. His family stood there with two, no, three other figures in dark suits. Policemen. All their faces were wrapped in puzzlement and utter shock. Never to accept. Never to accept what they had come upon.

The sight of the filthy boy covered in blood, sweat, and tears, on his knees, his clothes shredded to tattered ribbons and surrounded by the gigantic sprawled bodies of hideous gargoyles was unquestionably bizarre and unexpected. But it was right there for everyone to see, so what was there to accept?

His breathing under control, Gabe gazed

down numbly at his defeated hobby around him. They had fallen away.

He looked somberly at York. The dragon's head was cocked quizzically on the carpet, still glaring up at him. The eyes were back to their pale maroon. Gabe looked long on the others, reaching out to him with their wicked gnarled claws and raking up only rug. They had made the supreme effort and failed, barely. The Dragons Three were done. They had fallen away, mute, stagnant, never again to move.

With a listless expression, he turned his attention back to the rigid configurations in the foyer. He was blinking like a little boy who had just woken up from a very long and very bad dream. One of them detached itself from the group and advanced. It was Mom. But she was doing the breast stroke in the air. Gabe rubbed his eyes with the back of his hand and saw he still had the .38 in his sliced fingers. He let the empty thing drop and bounce.

He felt clean smooth hands on his battered face, and Mom was right there. He inhaled her breath, the scent of her lipstick and her fading perfume. Anxiety crossed her face. She saw everything but understood nothing. Gabe found his tongue. He had to tell her.

"I . . . won."

He began to sway and reached out for her, smearing her raincoat with blood and earth. He was taffy. A warm drowsiness gushed down over and inside him and it felt fantastic because he really needed the sleep. And now he could. Nothing else on this spinning earth was of more importance now. Just the sleep. Just the warm, thick, chocolate sinking . . .

* * *

Outside in the steely cold, the rain continued. It drenched all things over and over as it came down in dense, glossy blankets in the absolute darkness.

The sparrows clustered together grimly. They resembled carved wooden ornaments attached to the dribbling fence top. Their eyes were tiny glittering chips of black ice.

With what sounded like a whisper, the group of birds left the fence and whisked upward. They were pocket-sized kites whizzing through the frosty atmosphere, virtually dodging the drops of rain. Then, in silent harmony, the dark sparrows razored up, reaching for the boundless, twinkling heavens; reaching, reaching, reaching . . . and disappeared.

ATTENTION TEENAGE AUTHORS!
Lee J. Hindle's *DRAGON FALL* was the 1983 Avon/Flare Young Adult Novel Competition winner. You can be the 1985 winner!

Here are the submission requirements:

We will accept completed manuscripts from authors between the ages of thirteen and eighteen from January 1, 1985 through August 31, 1985 at the following address:
The Editors, Avon/Flare Novel Competition
Avon Books, Room 1204, 1790 Broadway
New York, New York 10019

Each manuscript should be approximately 125 to 200 pages, or about 30,000 to 50,000 words (based on 250 words per page).

All manuscripts must be typed, double-spaced, on a single side of the page only.

Along with your manuscript, please enclose a letter that includes a short description of your novel, your name, address, telephone number, and your age.

You are eligible to submit a manuscript if you will be no younger than thirteen and no older than eighteen years of age as of December 31, 1984. Enclose a self-addressed, stamped envelope for the return of your manuscript, and a self-addressed, stamped postcard so that we can let you know we have received your submission.

PLEASE BE SURE TO RETAIN A COPY OF YOUR MANUSCRIPT. WE CANNOT BE RESPONSIBLE FOR MANUSCRIPTS.

The Prize: If you win this competition your novel will be published by Avon/Flare for an advance of $5,000.00 against royalties. A parent or guardian's signature (consent) will be required on your publishing contract.

We reserve the right to use the winning author's name and photograph for advertising, promotion and publicity.

If you wish to be notified of the winner, please enclose a self-addressed, stamped postcard for this purpose. Notification will also be made to major media.

Waiting Time: We will try to review your manuscript within three months. However, it is possible that we will hold on your manuscript for as long as a year, or until the winner is announced.

VOID WHERE PROHIBITED BY LAW.